for my children

CONTENTS

Part One

PART ONE

REAP
VIOLET
HISS

The hair, growing forth from thine head, as the glass, unbroken, holds together the frame surrounding it; curls, unfolding the gentle streams of consciousness that are thine own rare truth. Fragments, passed, fragrant, fast as running stockings. Millipede, one arm under the other. Like marble, reinforced by a warm, soft lap; clarified, and rendered smooth, as abalone, whose sleek tongue, whetted and as ever, ready; made lithe though nimbler, still, than eagulls resting poised, inverted mid-air, thick as pea soup is as fog. The elk, huge as caribou, moose, or musk-ox, hyphened and mulled as cider over in the mind, glacier-trodden, fissure-fjorded, split, severed, cracked, slit; rejoined, congealed, through molding moulted; moulded thick, impalpable, impenetrable impass passed, filled full and cupped, runneth over, bubbling and bursting to blooming

The mountain now moved, pausing momentarily, briefly catching its breath, the breadth of it being so broad as to make quite difficult the rewatering of the rivers contained therein. However, it seems that as its health had not been for some time as well as it once was, it was only with great difficulty, and with such concerted concentration of effort and its energies that it was able to even lift itself a bit or budge an inch, having, immediately to collapse again onto the great mesa which had been its turf and stomping ground for all of this time.

Again and again it tried, but to no avail; each time it succeeded in raising its yeast with the great heat of its own body to such a degree of expansion that it would suddenly start and reel, collapsing into a bag of bones, a puddle of pebbles, a sea of sand, a dune of dust. Thus did it come to pass, that as the sun arose each morning and the moon in the evening, each descending with the coming and going of night and day, or day into night, respectively. Yea, even as each unto each, so do the seasons change the year 'round, even as life and death emerge and merge, so were the sands of time sifted as the mountains were leveled, each dissolved into the other, a sea of tears.

The air quivered; opening and wafting, pausing reluctantly, ineluctable as morning. Again, the split in the street opened, gaping; verbal and fertile eyes glaring, wide iridescent as phosphorescent minerals or night moths

Stellar; virile, and what does the difference mean between words' worth and levitation? Nervous, they fell asleep, fallen as oak, unpunctured; awake punctually with punctuation. The bird glides, dipping, eyes closed

Paper-thin like white birch peeled, strip mind scraped scooped popover I've lost my persimmon snatch found what a catch not by the chair of my chinny-chin-chin knot handle or thorn for's core answer vein ear sage oh

Far, the hands give way and bear ripe fruit. Before, stars tinkle an angularity not less fragile than agile midnight. Again, to sharpen the point, the image is double. Make no mistake: the vision, impaired, is by no means insurmountable. The extension, a welcome pilgrim come of age. The initial distortion, in the case of the upper, lowered in case the case was brought up. The finger-nail, watchful as dandylion blown away. The umbrella, opening wide as wingspan two abreast. The willow, whispering wishes, wooly and pointed, to the wall. Sweet, perspiration, sudden and caviar. Minor surgery, waterfall. The rude awakening, please. The raising of the sail: plunge, tilt, octagon, peel. Butter, whipped creamery sweet clarified lightly chasuble. The monument, bathed and charitable. The flower, deep and undated in. The rest, a pear and form you late of all a peace. A cloud, feather dusted as the wing of moth. Then, as ever wheeled through pin-like, fallowed, as the calm plain of ear drums, evening. Still, over albumen, philomel reseeds tender young shoots. Filled, the river swells and dips, peaks and ebbs. The warmth of tubers, running together, tied and dancing, spoons.

The white line lengthens, gradually grows, enfolding the enclosure of its own direction, sensing the balance, pivoted, irreversible, a masterpiece of understatement. Lithe, he hugs the road, molding his form to the curve of the other, while his road in turn bends its shape to embrace to mountain.

All Hallows Eve; the green, iridescent—I lay in my bed and tell little white lies. Everything I write is a false arrest. I should be suede. From the tip of my queue to the tip of my toes.

The night swelled softly. The twinkle in your eye. The bedclothes cling. I was reaching such a pitch that pearls of sweat dripped from my body onto yours. At the train, you kissed me good-bye and a hug. I've never been so startled.

I haven't dared write what I really feel, feeling my language has not the facility for expression of my thoughts; rather, I was afraid to try, fearing that I could really say what I needed to.

I'm afraid to think, I think. I notice now how I form my "k's" differently lately. In fact, the entire act of writing, the physical movement itself, let alone the content of it, has become inescapably conscious.

I am acutely aware of all the things I was able to ignore before, or at least was able to pretend I didn't see them. Certain things enraged me so. The thought of you with someone else. The thought of you with yourself.

Certain images were almost unbearably arousing: the thought of you asleep, in the shower, on the toilet, eating, listening to music.

Memories of the first times we were together haunt me. And how I couldn't call you those two months. Sitting on the windowsill, "If I hadn't come in onto the bed at that moment," sitting suddenly, our arms tightly around each other, do you remember these things as I do? I am afraid to know. But I want to. I want to know you, "One thing we must always do: we must always be totally honest with each other."

"I can ice skate, too."

I can hardly imagine that I am really going to see you in two days. What will it be like? What will happen? "I'm afraid that I will either want to be with you, or not."

I'm as afraid to be with anyone else as I am afraid to be with you. I want to be with you more than anything in the world. I don't want to be with anyone else. Certainly not at least after it's dark or after the sun rises, certainly not before it's dark or after the moon rises, certainly not after it's light or before the sun sets. Certainly not before it's light or after the moon sets. We're both full of hot air.

The photograph I carry with me in my notebook wherever I go, I look at occasionally. Just now in the bright light of the subway car I can see its true colors. I remember so vividly that last supper you said you were hungry but didn't want to cook (oh how our gestures symbolize deeper levels of consciousness, and give vent to manifestations of feelings unutterable in any other way).The foremost criterion for writing should be to fill up the white spaces, line after line, from beginning to end.

I carry the world around in my bag. I went home to get the key, having forgotten it. Now what am I to sharpen my pencil with?

I'd completely forgotten about that day at the museum.

What are you doing right now? Are you lying in bed too? Are you awake or asleep? Are you in you underwear or naked? Is your light on or off? Are you looking out the window? Listening to music?

You are on your way, en route; you are coming. But have you yet departed, or have you yet arrived? The base of the thumbnail bleeds. Slowly emitting a low moan, softly flowing, but soft: what light from yonder window breaks? It is the east, and you are the sun.

I swell up, my breast heaves oceans: the doors, open. Centrifugal force, centripetal horse. The fog lifts the acorns fall.

The safety pin holds the gold enfolding, the paint once removed only the ghost remains a mere shadow of that which that and more.

The light, golden in spurts streaks through the window of the train interrupts the beams the bridge erupts the blue are you now riding down the road the trees disrupt the rays of platinum before your very eyes of blue.

What are you thinking of? Are you looking out the window? Do you see anything? Is the window open? Do you feel the air? Does the wind blow your hair?

And, so when the light brick whitely smoulders eroding nest, shall pluck from angels' hair irascible, the eyelashes of Eden.

Motionless, verisimilitude; utter a single word—please . . . do not doubt an iota of anything. We do try to accommodate everyone. It is through this practice that nothing is accomplished.

I really want to say something. I really want to be able to say what I have to say, without being afraid.

I am not afraid, not now. I believe in this. With all my heart. Is it possible. That this is true. That it is actually real. You once said, "It's so real and beautiful where it is, why think . . . ?"

Everything is real and beautiful, perfect perhaps, which is never to say that it shall not continue and grow to be more so. This is and needs must be rather, an affirmation that is shall be so. It is so.

The morning after; riding on the train again. The air

is unusually clear, the day is beautiful. Wish you were here, although it's not difficult. That is, I feel a great warmth inside me. I am not without you.

The light amazes me. The green is startling. At breakfast, I discovered an insect inside my pomegranate. It was possessed of such a simple and gentle temperament, it radiated great waves of peace, slowly moving through the bright red fruit, a small grey dot walking along among the globules, translucent, seed-centered and swollen with sap, its flat pigmentation strangely camouflaging the little big, stoic in its steady determination, leading him on toward the pursuit of his destiny.

By the rules, a merry-go-round could get fuel, while a tractor stands idle in the field.

Here I am in bed again, thinking of you. It's cold outside; must be much colder where you are. It's after midnight. Are you going to call? You have to get dressed and go outside to a telephone. Do you remember?

It's so warm in my room. It's been such a lazy day. It's been such a sleepy night. The air is soft inside my room. I hear dampened sounds outside my window. The street is so quiet. Everything sounds so far away. The night, or consequently my life in this room, pressed beneath glass, crushed before the moth, pheasant under glass, a delay in glass.

The thin space between the glass and window frame emits a quiet buzz, occasional and unobtrusive.

I'm going to go to sleep now. I turn out the lights. I'm writing by flashlight. The window is buzzing. I'm tired. I feel easy though. Quiet. Full. I don't feel really sad that you didn't call, even though or perhaps because you said you would there is nothing to . . . but then, it would've been nice. Maybe it's better this way. Talking is really just so much talking anyhow.

I hope you're asleep. I like the feeling of us both asleep. Even though you're far away. We are together. Sweet dreams.

The entrails encircle; livid and it seems to be morning again. Are you awake? How much of that can you really understand? A sweater over this particular is not a good idea. We knew this all along and yet since the beginning, as suddenly as we're all out of a sudden doors.

Why did the chicken cross the road?

Why did the boy cross the bridge?

Why did the forest cross the fruit stand?

And why can't I escape the tyranny of my sweater?

I feel puritanical about pâté. That makes me feel so good. I want to brush my hair. Well, I write that down; why don't you? You would've been better off at home with an English muffin.

The window opened and clothed my eyes. Morning had come dotted and tea-crossed. Inconspicuously, the weather changed from this one will have two to this one will have won too, also.

The body disengages color forms and re-assembled, frees itself from the bondage of youth, a toothless grin.

Ox car desire named double that's good unheard an ox a head knocks ahead of ears unearth where every mind heeds exactly swelling tender tissues. Actually a sign, out of the well your legs without two ways, earn their keep. If you're caught, open the little eggs, tug them, stretch back your ankles, pull out to fit; they hug the hollows. Now the knees; eggs hold you without bagging. Eggs hug you, hold you, never let you go.

Hope from a hole of eggs. Eggs, Eggs; Queen and sheer.
Ummy to oes; ose. For see the eight-eight art the eggs.

> Oh, I wish I could give you everything in the world
> in 3 minutes or 3 seconds
> a jigsaw puzzle for adults,
> assembled by children; that's what I'd give you.

In the district of the red cafe light the billiards know
that bards brick would mould rest less white rest no
explosion so's to not accentuate for the fun of it by
mention of it by pure chance can you hear the willow
all night sometimes during the day the door a different
way, sitting around do you think the walls are curved is
there any explanation in with out with it

Sitting here is like remembering your telling of
that night you went to that place where you drank the
elements and there behind the eyes you lay, sprawling
on a couch I cannot imagine you in that situation stone
space and when the girl came over to you you said she
looked like a 42nd Street whore she spoke to you you
spoke she told you you shouldn't be so heavy you were
drifting away somewhere she roused you you were

not were you aroused I can't imagine the setting Jean Harlow are you or Leslie Howard which of which is but the red roof you really do.

There are are is there much to say that is just when it seemed there was nothing left there was everything in the middle of his forehead I'm dizzy sea sick air lift cotton seed oil the axis of my windmill. It's your turn now, velvet crushed orange intersection way laid. Enduring daylight lilies lamp-posts ate illumined by surrounding air as in the evening atmosphere made luminous by its extending limb and philtered through the night as the ink of the squid.

The feeling is as though something was (were) amiss; semi-colon without quite knowing why or where or when or whom not to mention how. The eternal spirals through the burning fiery furnace.

Willa Cather whether or not superimposed a posteriori post-mortem without being a matter of circumference as par for the Corsican equestrian, nothing again has been accomplished.

In the gloaming, oh my darling, the silence chirps,

pulsates in the present tense, taut untaught by any man but rather learned as knowledge acquired through the innocence of pre-natal concern.

Excuse me sir but you have a hole in your pocket and it looks as though your keys may fall out. Let me hold your packages. We'll manage somehow. Though the journey be arduous and the road be long, we shall somehow through perseverance does one further.

The orchard now in bloom, the birds in tune intone a gentle web of dew, as spiders hum their eyebrows rise as quivering branches leave their fall till autumn and as unto Til Eulenspiegel. It's hard to think of anything but you when you're all I'm thinking of.

The rose floats a word above the rest of the world. In answer to the very similitude of effervescence, versification leads toward and from the elocution.

Evening, the air bare, scarcely there. How many times has this been where I am. The only difference this time is in the way that the transcendence of similitude was reserved non-exclusively by the intentions of all concerned.

But now, the drops bubble. The bubbles drop, unreserved and entirely without second thoughts.

This somehow facilitates a spontaneous relation of nevertheless carefully derived conclusions.

There is really no longer not any reason for those things which before were inexplicable. The fartherland long once removed by the x-number of extra factors, now recognizable as being of definite form, within the larger scope of things.

How then, could we have ever imagined a decidedly different ordering of all we have come to know in the way we've come to think of it. It is not impossible to do differently now or at any other time prior to the change of season.

The way things when all is said and done, what is done and said. When all is done and said, what is said and done.

A line forms twilight, luminous and revelatory as a redefined coagulation in circumference of sensibility.

Mildewn, rusting oxidation re-evaluates realization without exception. The newly mown dune restfully sails across my visage, unassumingly, self-contained, re-instated as the first day of winter. How believable it seems. How flexible and afraid. Almost as though the only difference were certain as to the determinants of remembering. Regardless of the simultaneity of response either requested or sequestered, it would appear as though the only difference between here and there or then and now would be visibly discernable as being the only absolute parameter of measurement with which things might be made to be visibly discernable, in this way filtering the escape of novelty escaping the novel filtering as novelly as an escape of a novel through a filter.

This all of course leads to the eventual dusting of the inevitability of perpetuating a form of expression not entirely removed from its original intentions. This says without going that an arbitrary classification of our vocabulary might lead to the unnecessary compulsion of pharmaceutical reflexes.

This all indicating that as we formerly believed, the numerological ordering of our own destinies rejects seemingly a rescued portion of this conception with a clarity never before imagined.

The belief in this might be so strong as to overcome any persistence toward the contradiction of the cold air of evening.

I've always tried to write before I had a chance to think about it. That is not what I need to do now. I want to write what I feel.

Heaven band-aid reconcile outwardly eke reduce without cactus instill etch under than pressed real form ruin wilt risk wool orange turn through the octopus volatile insinuations extricate willingly varnished virility Corsican ventilators throughout the valley inundated rescued though goes beyond elevation that night of persimmon was coffee-filter tree stump volcanic ash surely related the stars surrender

In antiphony, the recent triads evaluate their hymnals.

It's not the snow that I'm after; it's what's under it.

The hose quivers; the heart plucks eyelashes. Irascible, as the new moon, "Just call me the Sphinx and forget it."

What is whiter than snow, likes to travel, and sometimes slants slightly toward the right quivering, unnoticeably? A renegade raindrop, when no one is looking.

What makes you think it wants to be caressed, when

in fact, all it really wants is a pedicure? A moose with a suspicious alibi.

Which tells the most veritable truth: a fortune-cookie, a lion-tamer, or a feather-duster? A filibuster, because it abandons welcome mats.

Where would be the least likely place to fall in love: the top of a pyramid, the lobby of a periwinkle, in the middle of a rainforest? Frescobaldi.

If I were to write and again, and then, if I were to write and then, and again, if I were to write oh when, would I see you again, anyhow, and when will I see you again?

When the trees sigh their whispering wishes, when the air wills its quiet refrain, when the sun sits there mooning all day and all night, then yet will I see you again and then, and then will I see you again?

Do you remember way back when, I started, startled, thick and thin, rationale turned outside-in, a sound forewarns what whatever

Time will tell. I intend to place all the parts end to end and descend into the depths of the cavity without looking forward. The periodic displacement of one thing or another can only indefinitely reward the loser for his efforts by relinquishing all claim to the proper person proper, properly. Why weren't you there? I had to contain my rage. The night owl catches the early bird catching the worm. The telephone strangles the recipient, smothering its object, it lifts lids; eyes thoroughly the nightingale up periscope. Tied to the bedposts, reeling as the howl of the wolf, winded, winds, wolfing down the howl, winding up the reel. The bird's eggs, flustered, speckled, speculate upon the fate of the fatherland. Inconsistent, the elephantine paregoric, replays intently the great old songs of yesteryear.

When you walked in, I mistook you for someone of a similar color but a logarithmic value settlement.

For how long can your body conceal the weight of its own proportions from itself, it seems that to others nothing is invisible; going where?

What does the implication of "How did it go?" mean? Did the inevitable rearrangement regain consciousness—how the earlobe did you do what in fact you never did in essence upside down the ink does not flow.

It emerged, gradually, as though we'd never known it was coming in the first place. Furthermore, as lightning intervenes, the flashback reveals a remembrance of embouchure totally forgotten.

The telephone tilted and solemn returns of evening rebroadcast reruns of things that were never made, nodes which never occurred, oculists who believed in salmon.

Umbrellas reverberate halcyon, salivary remains of a brief romp through the park. Initiates, we orifice to believe the beginning of inordinate exertion.

The moth-style egrets: that is to imply that maybe he has a lover? Test tube parabolas spurn the perambulator through the most triumvirate of examinations. When the end was reached, what did this signify? That perhaps in the same way that glass may slip off the ear what remains to be said remains to be seen.

The vortex contains the lock; is there a place this late that makes keys?

The seal, placed in the center of the card, returned a specific realization as though the hottest thing around . . . flying her hands like wings: four-hundred fifty horses. These are the hands, everything's so close together, I put my head in my pocket. My hands wore a heavier doubt. And then it becomes a long-haired star. This place is like a tomb between now and morning.

I'd forgotten why I'd stood up; remembering, bare-footed bravely crossed the room to the other side.

Is this what it was like? I don't feel lost. The bathroom is closed; I don't have to use it anyway.

The people here look so understanding, sensitive.

The nail file cracked its knuckles. Impossible, you say? Improbable, I say.

Where so you go they all in come and when in they you and where oh where do the pussy-cats go when it snows?

The trees melt: crystalized dew-dropped dry iced, love is on the table, eat your fruitful garden, open on contact. I'm looking at the wall, I don't see my fossil.

Do you promise? Maybe I can't promise. Well then, perhaps you'll change your handwriting. What if I change my hair style? Do you change your underwear? Would you ask me that in dissimilar circumstances?

Would you expect me to answer under different conditions? If things were, would, or ever could be the same again, might anything be recognizable?

As such, do you know what I mean when I say go and when you say stop? If I told you to go fly a kite would you understand what I meant?

How could you expect me to explain to you how I feel if you know already? Does it make any difference whether or not I answer?

Regardless of the explanation, does it concern you if I am concerned or not? Does it matter if I am finally able to say these things and do actually say them? How on earth do you expect me to go on like this? You've given me the back of my own hand.

I have nothing left to go on. Yet I keep going on. It makes no difference any more whether or not what places dawn to water or not to well.

There's this thing that keeps thinking of me that I keep thinking of. It's rather wishful thinking, somewhat like the pitter-patter of little feet.

Also, like a glove, ascending rakes the hair, the water nymph, solemn air, oh lip hold. The fox, recollected after many winters, swanlike, taverned, tureened, tourniqueted, derailed, misappropriated.

Is there any difference anymore between is there any difference and anymore? Is a blanket really as caressing as though snow? Could one suddenly be sleepy and then as suddenly go to sleep? Would it make any difference to you whether or not I maintained my life as it is now and has always been or rather choose to change for what it could or might be?

Would you notice if I suddenly released a great fury of butterflies through your eyes and filled your mind all aflutter?

Would you mind if I took great liberties such as to suddenly abundantly without notice water your hair with feathers, snowflakes, and real dew drops, so as to give you pause to wonder, "Have I really been dreaming all along, and only now just so suddenly woken up, and not as I'd previously taken for granted, and though I naturally was awake as my usual state of being and only occasionally would dream, can this really be true, could this truly be real? I'll pinch myself and see."

Whereupon you plucked between your thumb and forefinger a wee bit of buttock, and lo, the bullock you'd been reared its head with laughter ecstatic.

Returning home, outside the door, struggling with the lock, my key in my hand, the feet began slowly to melt into a puddle.

Inside the safe no sound; a painting become a hat rack, suitable for framing. The replacement of the bread. No reason, beyond the full need of filling the vacuum of space, fulfilling a common dream. I shall return.

Irrevocability of forced entry. Amount of oval may be adjusted to suit taste. Inexplicable. It is though, as though everything had been predetermined. We must somehow come to an acceptance of the state of things. We must trust butter.

A twinge in the stomates may be lichened to triangular lilacs triangular. If this would seem to indicate that worse may come to worse, then, indeed would one thing lead to another?

Does, extemporaneously, any of this trigger any spontaneous reflexes or reflection in your central archdiocese?

The birdsong displayed a great propensity for relating of fortunes to and from their respective diurnal nocturnes.

The songbird could twist you around its little finger. The only factor to which the invalid could be corrected as being of significance within the fabric of the continuity of the elements proposed itself to be totally unrelated to any of the riddles herein defrauded.

The seeming impossibility of anyone's having anything to do with the eventuality previously related, seemed to preclude the existence of something beyond the realm of rationality; beyond the call of duty.

It was through this that we came to finally comprehend somehow the truth of the grey matter.

The eye of the beholder blinked and festered through the throngs of air bubbles which persisted in common places their superimpositions over and over understanding again on the tips of the heads of their tongues, pickled, smoked, and savoured for its rare sponge-like hyphenation.

We all but lost our senses when, meanwhile, he, whose arrival we had awaited for all the time in the world, the responsibility seemed indicative of several previously incorrect presumptions, all have been taken for a ride for granted.

Before anything more is said do you have any preference whether the left or right

The . . . a good way to begin a sentence. Do you know something? I like you. It's as though nerve gas might serve to illustrate a set of similar circumstances. Would you mind waiting in the car? Are you going to bring along your little box car? Is that the point of all this?

When the little hand points here and the big hand points there, where are we?

To haunt the sleep of sheep. I awoke with tears slicing my cheek.

The inevitability of the return uncertainty of the platitudes of Juno. Recasting of the archipelago of mourning. Automaton of excellence revitalized through vestments of cholera. Therapeutic value of lethargic customs, Castor and Pollux remembering the joys of days gone by, of knights errant. I can't write, the vestibule, I'm too cramped. My stylus, noble without being over, Udnie, related Lop Lop as through the fields we go.

Parliamentary, the earing heard a voice unopened since dorsal remnants preconceived alligators' vestigial glands. Raucous, unrumored rused through rue and pennyroyal; myrrh, recycled fossiled Lawrence; the bridge; pause. Give saint head; relearn the sounds of yes'd her ear. Finally, we've been to all these. Change here

That's hopeful. It's hopeful. What's hopeful? This seems hopeful. How can you say such a thing? Don't forget to remember punctuation. It may be months, even years before the threads of sustenance weave themselves into a fabric through which we may see each other as we really are.

The gesture is purely speculative. The mirror is merely menstruating. The seasons are only arsonists. The fluid which flows within our instance yearns for asparagus in bed. The cold, fragile Artemidorus, reaches out to taste the substance of years throughout our inkwells. The pyramid is like an overturned vessel catty-cornered and salamandered, to the left and to the right, eager as the field starts to go.

. . . float like a butterfly. Think about it. Without thinking about it. Don't give it a thought. Nothing is everything is sacred. Not to mention even you. Don't mention it. No thanks but thanks but no thanks. Just like burnt umber. Say it. Burnt toast. Salted buttered salt. The new order of things asks more of us, unseen but heard, give second thoughts to our pause and trailing ewe. The frond grows ardour unable to explain what could be so simply said.

Turn around he said. I tried. That wasn't enough. The crisis had barely begun. But for now it would have to do. We wound it up and started all over again. Much to our surmise, matters were not so simple. This time around we were in store for some big dividends. We had chewed more than we could bite off. This time there is no going back. To be sure is for keepsake. All is as it should be.

Now, then. Does any of this make any sense to you? And if it did would that mean anything? Or, could it have been mistaken for something else?

Would we have noticed when they are going to watch birds? Did anyone turning the page I planned on surprised you are going to chopped the tree down it hits him under the head if you hadn't said timber she isn't going to took the hat off?

Shoots the fuzz-encrusted machine immobile will press the wrong button

Now, then. Perhaps we can get down to business. Had you noticed the way that the sky shone last night?

As far as you can see has a building collapsed when there is no one inside it? What does it mean to stir up trouble? Could it make any difference even if you go tell him to wait for us? Is continuity determined by more or less the same things as vertigo? Can you? What? Okay. What does that mean? Would you know it if you saw it? You could've blown me over with a feather.

My mother grew this from seed. My mother grew this in the sea.

An uneasy chair, an unsafe pin. Needless to say. When a flyspeck moves, it is doubtless the stitch in time of the final e. The finale, high tea so dumb and go more a bout with spin ach no loss or spinach con you tin us lie a crows n'est pass out in side reap eat Moses pad real would chew rust aardvark must eel on gat loose awls on savoy awning is leak a sin gull ear a king of leeks a single year a shingle locks a finger lacks ginger works.

The low limb angled pin egg rasp soot holed fin girt snailed wick stone an dive I've vine.

Stoop and does this any confluence toward the center of either up on or down hair re under again me thought it back words upstairs still and as though there were no reflection to begin with out of doors or in straight off the top of my head the drawers worth without words are speechless, none the less for in exactitude the regurgitation of the most fundamental instincts, no matter, the difference between the former and the latter may not necessarily be so highly detrimental to any or all of those concerned, there is none now nor ever was. However, this does not rule out the possibility of the future.

Seeing as clearly as we do the full scope of possibility is within our reach. There can be no grasp of hands without some understanding (if no one understands) then, well and what are is a place from dawn is which with watered what without it? The answer—there is none. The question—forgotten at no loss to anyone.

Signals turn about face abandon articles, unnecessarily so. The interrogation proved unprofitable, but not entirely worthless. He didn't know that you knew him. Did you know that?

Icicles, meanwhile, hang between his legs, immobile, mute, and unassisted.

What is the point if not pointless? Then, what is the point if not point less? If what is the point then not point less? Not what is the point of then point less? Question the point if not then less. Then of the point and not less than?

How long could this go if on whether he or she or it did or did not make any difference if in or out of or in fact bewildered by the coming attractions burnt out bulbous out chimera not receptacle bewildered of course as as participle caught not endangered din of partridge in the middle of formation of light patterns return if opened found curl vent if saline to sad bee tree toot eyes elf urn said, "oo!" he laughed, "ow!" ease.

Calculate the depth of desire to relive the life of October; the arbor is over. The dream is over. The iceman cometh. The air is green and where. Les enfants du paradis. L'encre du chine. C'est ca. How come, well you know. Is it as important as you think to keep a close chronicle daily of all events transpiring? The best time to write poetry. There is no time like the present. The gloves make you stop and think. The page on the opposite side is blank. The red shoes, you know, the one with the cuirasses. It is in you. It is you. To be alone and happy and able to write with gloves on. Able to leap tall heartaches in a single bound. Nothing but heartaches.

Except January. That is no exception. I accept. Before dawn, the buzzards bay.

Faint sea licks, an unemployed alchemist, like codfish, aires says fro me these

If not white, then the closest thing to it. It's good for them because it keeps their carpets.

She came running after us with a Tyrolian loudspeaker. It was the same again just like the time when we the eggplant anymore couldn't. The eraser rebutted and searched deeply for a reason in answer to a question which had not yet been asked. The q-tip long forlorn gone with the going of coming, once moist, now evaporated, lustre-lost, lips empty lip stick cases, or pre-natal, like unsharpened pencils. Pardon me. Disenchanted, or elastic, loose hanging untaut. Oh yes Ezra, swoop down on them like an eagle from the sky. I feel like such a fool leaving here as big as I came in. You can turn off the radio but you can't turn off the voice of God. Good-bye dear, I do hope you find him soon. Misery loves company. Well we're here. You're the best friend I ever had. The same old house, the same old room, miracles. We should all be sand. You shouldn't be in a place like this. I am as the strength of ten men. I am receiving you. Nice room near Brighton twenty quid a week who wants it. I told you to go before we started now you can wait till we get there.

He's asleep. I wrote it down for you. The chicken's nice and juicy. I want to start living right with you. I don't know. Month after month. Isolated, alone. All over the world people are moving like sleepwalkers. Are the stars out tonight? You two men take the wall over there. Is he gone? What am I doing here, what am I doing here? May be the last meal you'll get. We have gathered together not in fear but in love. I'm going with you. What are we going to do? We're going home. Honey, we'll get a million dollars of publicity out of this. I mean it is finished, isn't it? That's why you're home.

Involuntary servitude of the kitchen reminds one of the days of ages long passed since we came to know the difference in between the first last, and next at last, alas. The turn of phrase rebounds throughout one ear and in the other there is no divergence point identifiable as absolute with respect to one ore the other cross teas with me. Will you please give me some indication of something, give us a sign, something to stop and go on with.

The wind will mill the vespers force the sea to voice the whispers in turn intone in tune. We open with the overture. Surprising, isn't it, the way the wind weaves worlds without wishes. Trees do not open and close softly or otherwise enfolding and or re or and spreading the wings or arms and leafy green or otherwise palms in any sense or shape or form.

The answer is simply not that simple. Whether written or spoken words do not betoken necessity so. Explicitly, he watches from the mountain doors. Keep out of reach. Dew rose up from the ground. The white owl sits, the new-mown hay. Twice or thrice around. Warming is my prince. Did I say warning? Morning? Who is he? Did you talk to anybody?

The sage restores nonviolence, perpetrating incest. The dust for a change. Did you ever?

Bending my head, I lower my upper lip into the cup. I feel the foreign presence in the warm liquid. It is as though my lip touched itself.

All of the essence of you is in me all of the essence of me is in you all of the essence of me is in me all of the essence of you is in you all of the you of you is in essence me all of the me of me is in essence you all of the you of me is in essence you all of the me of you is in essence you all of the you of me is in essence me all of the me of you is in essence you all of the you of you is in essence you all of the me of me is in essence me.

Your tree. Winged and moon struck.

However, do you understand what I've been trying to tell. It's like this there is no difference within out the ordinary light of the arc light. The century relies on values which are obsolete, and meaningless. The slippers, ragged and crumbling. It's like my body still tells me things. Likewise, if you were in trouble I'd try to help you.

I left him at home in bed with several best-sellers he had assembled variously for the day's reading. Soon they will be gone and the city will be safe again. I asked him if he wanted to come along to church. He said you must be patient. I fucking knew that kid. The music left me with much to be desired.

It did not satisfy any deep needs; I guess I must have great needs. A young man grown old. How many times can you go over the river before the bridge breaks? What bridge? Why did the road cross the bridge?

If bed is a place you have to go there to get to, chances are you'll never make it.

The tide is to run myself down until I fall asleep. The ink eye'd in keys pied or when tip these pout egg on. Our toe'd ant hall ogre eye amp'd hem answered intone in are toad whose beast charred isn't Moe's elf. To so sigh at tea, art owed wasn't addict adamant many wasp been who's so weave the trees toga they're rebound woven together their woe vine to gather there woof in said on to another, there is no difference I can see if you asked me I'd say it's all the same in the beginning or the end, it really makes no difference where or when.

To which the sun might think it queer to have so sudden slumbered here while their visions disappeared.

We concede to numerological insistence, thereby dividing intention from will-power, entirely unsatisfactorily, we resolve to extract our next off kiln are vin oven wreaked of have or half forget-me knots my minds' eyes' false lashes cat of nine tales respond surprisingly well when regarded in the light of present circumstances as they appear to exist in this situation.

Practically invisible, for our purpose, non-refundable

the fundament mentally funded filament refunded fundamentally misconstrued from the beginning, hand over hand through the fields of yellow corn.

How about it? Well is a place from which is drawn a watered dawn? A suppository: it's part of a carburetor.

Oh, jaundice! Oh hounds that sing! Oh pores which rage ravishing of the sort, the source of all previous misspellings. The question of singularity or plurality is so far out of date, it's pathetic. As far as the extent of which I remember when I couldn't get you out of a white shirt, stiff as cardboard, unreal. Extraordinary, isn't it how one may resume the red tie with a plaid sport coat?

Thus, thus, what is thus? as though we'd forgotten to remember.

Still, the eaves wander, penitent, though uncrossed, however bedraggled, the question remains, unanswered. Soft dominion, reunite our arbors, calculate incubation, receive results of suggestions made and unmade, warn and watered, sylph self man. Rinse evenly while

Needless to say, the reply was not without eloquence. The clock tick-tocked

Yes, the hours altered, we proceeded to contract many reasons for accenting anything.

Trance we chicks then oar dirred will terred in ordered we ill turd I n'aught erred wheel'd heard I nor'th red wee altered I n'ought read we'll all'd her

Seeing is believing, as clear as day. The light of morning, the fixity of windows, the clarity of space defining air, the distance between two things being equal only to the space needing to be traversed to get from one to the other, or rather, the ratio of time times the effort required to accomplish transcendence of physicality in terms defined only by definition as being indefinable, in terms of any clarity possibly conceivable as being possible more than likely as well as not on a purely conceptual level, thereby traversing all physical parameters, transcendent only by refusing to hide.

Although this procedure may not of necessity necessarily bring one or two from point A to point B and or, even, depending on the deepening of wounds, open, opened, opening and or closed to point to or toward and or towards ultimately to lead one to finding oneself suddenly or slowly through a period of time arriving, about to arrive, or having arrived at point C.

At this point it is or could might or conceivably be considerably difficult or present considerable difficulty as far as any attempt might go toward the ultimate goal of definition of the parameters of any given situation. This remains to be seen. OK. Yeah. All right. Alright. Journey to journey man almost made it. Gone now forever the difference was made clear. The only explanation had been given the courage it took to enter the room. The fire. False alarm. Why are they oscillating, then? It would be nice if that were true. Except, there was a full moon out, wasn't it? The center caved in, determining a texture unmistakable for any as thing being else. It was only after several moments that I noticed the various activities occurring in the room. I tried to speak, opening my mouth, no words came out. I took off my shoes off. Again, a breeze. It feels like you're creating something. Well you are. Strange, how the most morbid depression can suddenly turn inside-out.

Like a thread, thread-like, the thread emerged from the floor, through the carpet. Then what? Is this the way everyone else is? Does the addition of a question mark signify an adherence to aboriginal instincts?

Then what? Well, there might easily have been a drowning, but there wasn't. You see, we might have tried to save the ship before it sank. However, due to the sudden change in the weather or not there might or might have not have been anything to salvage to begin again and or end with this time found our salvaged frond our savage friend retrace our steps as unbeknownst to us or anyone else for that matter. So what but. Leeks. Arranged, flowering the same way I do.

Now the fire, bounces rebounds too much really there for the asking, actually, the moon, reverberating throughout the evening, mystifying, as memories of silhouettes across the earlobes of albatross. Connected within the openings of orifices cancel all orders pre-post paid. Can you give me concrete evidence of proof of this? If not, why not? Then, we ask you do you go to remember the end with out to re-turn forth with an e and all for cast out of in or all re-bound aries.

It's incredible, it's like talking to the wall.

We strove toward neutrality. We made great strides toward neutrality. Complement my efforts with reciprocation. We made great motions (toward neutrality). We took great steps. We knew whereof we spoke.

To make motions in the direction of neutrality is not necessarily what is to be desired. The idea of neutrality seems to imply an indifference or inability to make a decision or to put into action one's thoughts or needs. It is possible that neutrality may only be achieved by experiencing the expression and expressing the experience of all aspects of any given situation or continuity of events; hence, the whole is equal to the sum of its parts.

It is perhaps through this procedure that a desirable reconciliation of all the elements of a state of being may be united.

In the interim, in terms of the lineage, the linear measure twelve times the size of any possible difference which might be observed to be reserved for all concerned. Confidentially impartiality determines survival, partially due to the similarity between because of and due to.

How now bow down below the winds blow themselves to sleep, reap violet hiss, backwords running

the minutes flash past each other moments passed too
fast already gone to catch with down up right flesh left
foot pod gone for way a good but or this for time sure

Sparrow pear put bare beauty write with out wishes
form you late of yonder veil mount a hundred sun set
thunder eyes attain moon rise.

At water's edge the pale green tide rebounds too soft
too oft' to ebb and or flow down load oun flat fear less
warned be worn and warmth undone their sown lion
weight awfully there sewn lean wait off lea the reason
Leoun way two fly.

Where now the bell hit the head why didn't it happen
then? The sewn mill dwindles as the air fallen Astarte
isn't it funny how once we

PARTING
THE
CURTAINS

At last all that remainders decapitates the will to order re-evaluations requires of certain of us various differentiations which we were no longer familiar with. The statement exacting the same re-enactment as the first expressed in our fundamental originations, we were perplexed to note the decidedly upward trend which our brend had noticeably projected, unintentionally defending the right of way which had meandered here before today, let's say it made its presence known to us as though nothing had ever been taken for granted as being of significance prior to the displacement of viable phenomena.

It is through the direst application of these procedures that it became quite clear to all concerned that there was no longer, nor had there ever been, any excuse for the reason of which we could had not and would in all likelihood be unable to predict any knowledge of whatsoever until after the actual fact of its occurance.

The miss-spelling which impregnated unnoticeably the structure of our intentional unconsciousness, which, stylistically differed in no recognizable way from the methods commonly employed in past circumstances of decidedly similar situations by our predecessors, were forcibly once removed from the context of their original parameters, took on a distinctly varied appearance when beheld momentarily from that particular vantage point which most complemented its parsonage.

The ardour, implicit in the redundancy which propagated the usefulness of this fictitious foetus which formerly had fed upon the feces of and about faced fisticuffs, engulfed now, in the frontage of its forced failures, was now and then relegated to indulge in the so similarly banal tortures of which we had all become so accustomed to.

THE
MIRROR

Parting the curtains, she gave a hoot to whom it did not matter, for that was not the point. What was important was not, that is, that was not the point. The parting of the points imparted a pointless impudence to the entire portion. Portentous, though the importance in no way pulled strings to which imps might doodle maliciously, whether or not the point was crossed, what came across was what was seen and not heard. Pointless though it seemed, the importance of imparting this partition, put pointers toward the pulleys of which we were impetuously precursors. Pull the point across, he said, and with a pat on the head, he suddenly distinguished between the forms which had before been so formless, which now, though the difference was not exactly clear, had made themselves apparent in a way, perhaps, that he had never before been able to see. He laced his shoes and faced the door.

Five years before the mirror broke the door had been replaced full-length and fitted to restore the exact dimensions of its original frame-work to bring the thing replaced the origin of its original need, the reason being a re-evaluation of its custom-made evolution; elegantly elocution could no long re-solve the predictability of predilection nor were any of the precautions which had been taken as prerequisite to the attainment of any goal or oriented success-story it became more and more apparent that there were things beyond which one could venture, but rarely, and if so, then subtly endure.

So? What to do. His scissors cut out paper dolls of his bedclothes. So what? The turtles'-doves which slowly moved off the wallpaper did not disturb his reverie. Sew what? Was there anything which would disrupt his conceptual reality now and here? Now and then. Dizzily, his fortitude was fragmented, and wearily he resolved to resign himself to the truth that thrust first his footing afar, through the foreign dust which collected densely across his field of vision.

CUMULATIVE KNOWLEDGE

I wish I could collect my thoughts the way some people collect and pin dead butterflies through the heart, stilled in flight, caught unawares, the unprepared-for emergency for which we all live and wait, lying under in state all aflutter, till dawn recoils the fawn at sunset stills the air, poised mid-air pressed unduly pierced the marrow culled apart the only change in weather or not water is what or watered not

The animal insistence which seems of necessity to replenish itself regularly without reference to conditional reflections or axioms pertaining to or not to anything conceivable within the realm of abandonment within closely from the outside inside locked key loss car correction

The(se) anima(l) instincts open doors already clothed to the cold enough air of even in night I'm over rest peel asleep foreign quotients still order stir conglomeration of consolidation next what there always is

Balance(d) petrifaction never seen without deliverance isn't never read book.

Living a legend there are some who will disconnect
there are some who will empty some who will reconsider
who will

There is a clarity that is the melting of a moth or the
buzzing of a lamp which turns out to be a fly caught
inside trapped to death the benefit of burnt umbral
clouds often grey with out an a at Pentecost Titania the
29th descends the waterfront uncovered as though to
let bygones go be gone bygones or orgones dissuaded
without cause of effect or pause and reject without
notice merely

Novitiate only notable not only for the innocence of
bystanders know no table no ton leaf or the innocents of
any possible difference on your part or my duplication
water under the bridge

He who commands the change of season must follow
down corridors and open windows

She who draws absent conclusions in the face of
congruent collar starchers needs must befit

The handmaidens who set tables laid bare by
heartless trailing ewes

In retrospect the difference was horizontally
convalescent with respect towards all and any and all

divergences from which we may be said to have changed descriptions from the superfluous to the supercilious in less than more than one breath.

The bite from which emerged slowly the only onetwo within reach which would have meant to have been planning a maneuvre of this sort since time expired. The capsized comparison combination of foresight, initiative, and destiny, might be simply emerged as an eloquent memory of something not quite of the realms with which reality necessitates comparison between it and itself and anything else within reach.

The science of deportation defied what would seem to be the only way out through self-criticism, foresight, ingenuity, and joie de vivre.

Seeing as we are within arms' reach way below the orifice of the ocean captivating on the rocks we were suddenly tugging at their feet having tried to invite danger and court dust feathers.

Cumulative knowledge again as indefinable as the difference between day and night though this time the variance toward which we could better serve our feelings having to sharpen our being without hurting within reason that doesn't mean anything from where you come in as I don't know because I haven't been here

I've run into dead ends I've been discovering things all the only time I'm sitting here I don't know in me I see a tight knot into which I cannot go walk out where you've been I do not know I can understand when I'm shaken I can walk outdoors how can you know it's something between you

As sigh late eyeing surface dents in the outer world isn't it peculiar how they stay at the bottom and know when it's time to come up for air. Perfectly under normal conditions standing face to shoulder the wind penetrating whole the breeze between the eaves; for shadows we send our lives which are taken away as erasers should be the only one who would know the change of movement the grace of the space of the graces of the space of graceful spaces and special graces or glacial ages, again the minimum effort is portrayed without as typecasting within central solstice glandular extremities defy equilibrium the definition of the thing itself by its own terms.

I am striving in hallways to corner states concentric conscious worldliness which precludes all possibility of persistence in arrangement of those aspects that vary to degree of common distillation.

When I am gone away the only thing I deem unnecessary is without intentions I'm getting sidetracked. The leaves are there toward which we constantly return reverting revisions from whence we came, grey and earth-trodden accompanied by tolls of trespasses in the night we alter our eyelids avert hourglass overt in every aspect save the soul-torn husked precaution star-laden foresight long forlorn thrust from where we watched our vantage point toward our desire soil-surfaced vestibule impoverished snail

Night of cloudless nights, I thought there was honey deadly nightshade, where there wasn't any it's always the same thing over and over again the unexpected euphemism, unknown euphoria comrade in arms, unarmed; yourself—leaves pressed leaves left pressed between the leaves: hidden from sight unmistakable vision clarified again tortured rhythm blinded casually release from withholding glorification cause to feel imagination separate discernment unequivocally dented circumscribed without forebodement the most life-giving conclusion as yet monumental repercussion further enhanced by unusual affluence because we might have forgotten.

Any number of countless purposes might have equally served as an excuse for the discontinuation of our inevitable disenchantment to lead ultimately to disenfranchisement from what exactly one could not know, precision not being our most prominent feature, in actuality the other way around from whichever way this might be said to be the other way around from.

The clouding over of hunger possibility might serve us better in the bedroom than here in the privacy of your own hail-storm over the inestimable value judgement for which we must be accepted as being responsible; however divergent our intakes may be or not discern that which might dissuade or disturb us from attainment of the completion of that which we know to be the only full expression of our most heart-felt surrounding inclinations one could serve to express several experiences within the context of the most similar of circumstantial disturbances carefully collecting all possible combinations of which we might be taken totally unawares the sound of the voices of which might reflect certain congruences of expression the most susceptible to which might unexpectedly turn out to be what we would have least expected from those to whom we would have been indebted and without the assistance of we surely will begin the final no unnatural stop particular train blend shoot of turn without my nest clock fall often slew impression demonstrate caliber question unimportant couldn't thought fortunate since deft total ability known as conscious vigilance reclaimed purpose difficult to define might not be so inflated were not detained by fact of conference through many labyrinths of sightless tortures my moans keep sentry forced bland confession tested starting eloquence we might at least accept our right to determine almost lethal starfish.

Without knowing it, they no doubt nearly always wend one's way through various ailments toward which no one escaped the characterization through whom I might run to some startled fawns to freeze their thrust which was of my own doing there could be nothing to explain to my satisfaction the sense of mild earthen foundries.

Gazing absentmindedly for a change don't we ever resolve any part of it; the only difference seems to be additional separation: silent unity speaks with what resources are to its advantage placed not and too soon to close whatever windows may have been left open as is said in rain days not divert attention from within and yet, our gaze returns do you remember the time you forgot didn't you—already, you know what I mean.

The grass, it was that was not what I meant. Anyone would only have to look at you to know. When I say you remember does that mean that I do, having already known what your answer would be would I have gone on, questioning anyway, I could have said something different, but would you have understood what it meant to me.

Barely begun, certain brave beliefs. As yet unknown as well to myself as to you, this goes without saying. This is second nature, what are we going to do. Somehow omission of consciousness leaves one to one's own devices. I recall a day when there was nothing in existence, quite simply speaking, nothing is ever the same twice. As far as redundancy is concerned, there is only so far to go; when one has been there, what is left to do. That remains to be seen what cannot be heard. Well within the boundaries of physicality, what remains without our knowledge cannot be expressed within the usage commonly employed for that with which we are no longer familiar.

What needs must most to be being said had best be abandoned without reservation given up the fleeting memory of the impermanent moment for which we grasp unerringly to learn what we may without the commitment required of more formal approaches towards the same experience for which there are so many names, identification of which would seem as an affectation—a reference point with which we could well do without, an additional anachronism within the boundaries of conceptual reality spectrums through which all things must pass through our eyes which however inaccurate, persist toward that which they hold as unmovable, constant, never inaccurate posture of things to come, that which exists now, and all having been through all the aeons of endless eternal humdrum.

The present moment, by which we mean that which is indefinable; ever changing, constant variance of ongoing definition, cancels all previous engagements, distinguishes between the named and the unnameable, timeless and spaceless, finite and infinite; perhaps the only accurate consolidation of flexible stability within the realms of convenience; that is formed of a need, however inaccurate of a fulfillment of a conception of existence as consisting of comparison of things within a framework of organized thought, rational convergence, particular patterns, seemingly reliable essential values, in which any phenomenal materialization could conceivably function within relation to its aspect in accordance with the sum-total of theoretically actual experience.

Consequently, the beginning and the ending merge and emerge as one within the relation of truly functional activism—there is nothing obsolete, all is consistent and in accordance with itself and through this everything else—there is essentially no distinction—anything within the classification of the realms of differentiation, including the conception of differentiation itself, is a pure arbitrary objectification of perception within the eye of the beholder, who, in perceiving anything as distinct or separate from one's self or one's self from anything has removed himself from the picture, or has hung the picture on the wall— he is out of the picture.

Thus, identification with any distinguishable exertion of energy force exterior or interior to one's personal frame of reference creates by the very recognition of separateness an ocean of self-alienation.

The thing beheld through the eyes of objectification becomes as it is defined through the conscious mind of the beholder—actually, nothing has changed, not the object of perception, but rather, the subject which has perceived.

Out the window the skies the birds flying home early but the roof close the door the barn the children which way did they go dark the birds mouth their beaks he had some somewhere careful am I where but oh somehow the steps upstairs the dress the clock Louis XIV configurations mindless of the necessities implied by caretakers, "Allow me the privilege, permit me do me the honor," where are you taking me don't jump, don't do it, I can't remember, floating above myself I saw myself was there a telephone, I don't remember, snow? waiting to go, my brother, carry me down upstairs, I don't know what's the matter, father, the fish? Fountain, suddenly summer, where are you, I am waiting for something I don't know what it is, this house. The bird eats itself. Remember, there are others waiting outside to get in.

You must have lost touch somewhere along the line you're out of bounds—if you pretend to think you do not know the way I feel or what I mean to say—mon bel jardinière? What do you mean I

told you so? It makes no difference to mean what you save your face for a rainy day or fall flat on it—crushing any possibility of future recognition. I don't care that there's no one on this train besides you or I—the forced-fed Matterhorn stuffed to the gills, the vehicle for what we might hesitate to call sanitation. The sign on the wall indicates a desirability to return to former practices, long forgotten, now hastily recommenced, in the heat of winter, our only defense from ourselves being that which remains invisible. Do you see the point? I can explain no more clearly now. This is all I can do.

I spent the day picking wildflowers along the side of the highway, going my way? There's little difference between the two when you come to think of it—what's the matter—can't you speak English? Don't you recognize me?

LIKE FOOTSTEPS HEARD FROM THE FLOOR ABOVE (DOCILE INTENTIONS)

D^{ear—}
As I have just finished speaking with you on the telephone it seems natural that what I am about to write is in some way intentionally or unconsciously directed toward your ears (you).

May we observe as a presupposed or preconceived pre-requisite or presumption that what one is writing is ultimately directed toward someone (else)? Is this observation relevant? As, even as I write, I pause before to formulate my thoughts, and thereby my words, thereby losing the train of thought—backing away, fearfully hesitantly, dis-uniting my self-consciousness from spontaneous combustion immediate reaction (the pause that refreshes?) losing touch, breaking the chain, tying myself up, refusing to let go, stopping and stopping again—it becomes a matter of an ongoing state of constant pause, punctuated occasionally by brief spurts of reflected stimulae, at this point totally removed from their original source and void of all inherent life force, motivation, or intent—dead things which do not exist within even the slightest realm of purpose; an essential breech of promise.

Like footsteps heard from the floor above, they

betray themselves, violating all they touch and all that touches them. No false advertising, no corn starch, no whimsical monstrosity. When the clicked mistake rest auk there's no one to blame but ourselves. To pursue the point any further is purposeless. Distant laughter, a far cry from what I expected to hear.

Forget it; let's pretend it never happened, which will be rather hard to do, since in fact it never did. Do you see the severe implications this could have? If you do, please tell me about it sometime, since I can't see a thing. The only thing I ask is please look after the children, and take care of yourself. And sometimes, at night, when the walls hang low and the windows threaten impossible visions, don't forget the star that melts tears to dreams, false affronts loose foothold, clear water pulls valued estimations from the depths of hieroglyphics through statutory vestibules, confident in their torsos, and dormant without seeming indignant.

Meanwhile, I wait . . . the days pass one through the other, a spiral slowly consuming any instinct toward competition; there being no precise detention used to rescue lost trappers. An appeal has been planned to prove the device used in cahoots with the other side, had employed devious and highly questionable suspicion along with a dusting of suspicious questioning.

Docile intentions tend to subdue the memory of an event before it occurs, thereby inducing

ALTERNATIVE LANGUAGE SYSTEM

Formulate and employ directly the (a) usage or words totally removed from their commonly accepted context (syntactically, grammatically, etymologically, definitively, conceptually, contextually)—establishing a continuity of language entirely removed from any rational attempt at explanation within the confines of traditional communicative terms—Attempt to achieve the attainment of a totally automatic integrity of verbal abuse—create an alternative language system employing estrogen, wallflowers, and tickertape—

Night, the inverse of the square route in trinity pictured as insatiable within mortal enclaves. Avoid what happened if it means that much to you. Stay where you are. One dissolves through blank elevations closing door behind, making sure there's a way back in; the thrift shop where one is paid for memories and porcelain.

The broken bed, saved by kindled young steam-mallows, set off by reserve forces, constant in large doses with the end in sight. The arms of the chair touched, momentarily paused, and breathed, heaving a sigh of relief, the only unsoiled pair to be found, our own undoing. It's so hard, I know, until you do it.

Alright, so there it is/was—cut it out—put it away—
go into the bathroom and write about it—

so what—you think you're the first—the only one
who has one—who are you trying to kid—sure, the
ceiling caved in—I know—I put my foot through it—
climb on up—

I can't quite capture the moment—Our central
nervous systems define the experience of heat, in the
process of air filtration, the means by which some
might save it for a rainy day?

————there's none so rainy, I'd say
save today's saving grace to save face, you say?
try the washing machines, instead.

RATIONAL THOUGHT

On on to the other to the other take me across take yourself across there is no reason to skip over my head can't wait for my body to catch up there is no where to wait nothing to wait in no soap box stand on which table sat no unnecessary weight from which to emanate, then it really gets too hot and it gets too late and before you know it there is nowhere left to go and then there is no more there there never was these terms do not apply my fingers don't comply although they do agree what shapes are formed and what forms shaped horizontal expressions of certain inclinations no less illegible than the others first last and not excluding anyone.

What I am trying to say may require a great effort on the part of my conscious mind that which is distinguishable not only by the method customarily used for situations such as these there is something charming about this all, something not entirely invisible to the naked eye, instead of enjoying ourselves, why not just forget it ever happened.

The balcony, the moon—the sound of the ocean; I can still hear it. The wind, the salty ocean breeze the air cold and wet, slicing our cheeks.

The walk on the beach the sensation of the sand underneath our feet. You didn't know that I felt it too, did you?

Turn out the light, close the window, draw the curtains, lower the shades, turn around, close your eyes, hug me. I wish I was a blanket or a pillow or an entire bed, better still, I wish I was your body, which is not you, to be able to cause your sensations. Imagine, punctuating your physique with subtle nuances which would not be thought of as foreign or external to your being, but totally taken unawares, unexpected, unplanned. I'd forgotten the birds too.

I hear melodies where there were motions the song undisturbed before the breaking of dawn stayed unmistakably straight without the same circular test tube as we has formerly been using for different purposes. By former standards, what was normal by former standards, like an echo removed from past suspicions, was like the inside of an ancient concept derived through constant inference toward distinct variation. Subdued for certain, the armor of descent turned out to be the only voice through which crossing washed the ton in Delaware.

Meanwhile, my only defense against my self-captivity while the untying of a shoe encourages the significance of an apparent gasp while swaying back and forth on a stool rattling along with the sound of a radiator heater like a crackle of a microphone and sudden crash—something is wrong with the piano.

Staggering along alone, the sound of the machines humming too many "m's," clip-clopping along the same drop cookies the rubbing of a seldom frequented usage like scratching at the door the non-existent pussycat purrs and breaks its way hurrying through the thick vegetation.

The richness of the scattered suchness quickly ended the oddness of squeezing of spinal occasional softness with a slight air of non-simplistic vastness of aerial bliss. Through which the rain ran hungrily past those frightened ones who push horses out of the way of passing vehicles distinct from previous attempts as yet unqualified as an explanation of what we were afraid to recognize any attempt to refill our orders throughout the attempt to rearrange our eyes.

Is this what do you hope it is or it isn't? How do you know what I mean when I say a little goes a long long way—is there no difference between fronthand and backhand—something suspicious about the former and auspicious of the latter. I can no longer keep my eyes open.

Where have you been all these years, I asked myself the same question; oh you really make me wonder. Where have you been all these years, and where are you going to be all these years? Where have you been keeping yourself? Where have you been keeping yourself with what? What have you been keeping yourself with? With what have you been keeping yourself? How have you been keeping yourself?

You make me stop and wonder how I've lived without you. You give me cause to pause and wonder how I've survived. You lead me to consider the manner with which I have managed to exist in the world without conscious awareness of your presence.

Now that you are here nothing will ever be the same again. Since you are here nothing is going to be the same. As you are here, everything is different. Now I know where you are, everything is going to be different. Now that nothing is going to be the same, is anything not going to be not different, and anyway, what does different mean anyway, so it should work out well enough so long alone.

The room the room feels like it's going to take off to take off going to take off what is this going to take off when going take off taking what off going what going off taking when going take off

Enough of this my glasses fall off—the room feels as though it's going to take off; the wind is blowing so hard outside. I wish I knew where you are—I wish we were with each other in the same place same time.

I wonder what you think of me, really—I mean beyond all that—that's all extraneous anyway—it has nothing to do with anything.

This is like a hurricane—I can't believe it—she always said "I can't believe it" or "I don't believe it." The wind is knocking at the window. He said hello.

The heat the heat but you know what I mean please be your heart. Come within I looked one morning your soul the mystery the beautiful rare wherever I don't yes I do however I try the only thing there it is. Remaining.

Lost lost lost lost—where? are you? Were you surprised to see me? I did not know I was being watched—did not realize I'd been recognized until it was too late—that night on the roof—who are you?—The sound of your mouth just being.

Node out is an him or hand I part hat an' eye ton tear who forward out his hound o' fjord oat

Pray the gust the sleeping gust I want to hold you in my arms all night through I want you

Me I'm amazed I can't live without someone—how? 's that? well you know everyone needs someone and if that someone was ourself, then we wouldn't need anyone—obviously that someone is not ourself—is it enough to know that that someone is not ourself—is it enough to free one of the self—when one is free of the self if one is still one then one is not yet free—the only thing to do is to be more than one since we cannot be less than one we are more than one and what is more than one—two?—if two is one and one then they are still one—one must be more than two—not necessarily three—one must take on a new existence through (with) another—thereby—two can and may be more than two ones.

WIRELESS
MESSAGES

Who knows who you are—calm flying night mist—not I—though I search far and wide my words lead me astray—

With great care—the ashes are moved away—the stardust clothes mercy through the veins—nothing dissuades further intuition like fortitude the frogs—or were they crickets—I can hear them now as I write— just like that night walking down the road. We stopped to listen—night peepers—the danger of rain—rising of the salt—which is closer—yours or mine—the time does not exist—and space—the heat rising from an oven—the squeeking of the table I am writing on— the shortest route from one place to another—which do you think is better—the distance between us—the color green—the eyes close—suddenly there you are in the window—the stars point the way—close the book—this is no accident.

I know what it is—I mean I am sitting here—am I not—I am supposedly a sentient being—No—steamed up my eyeglasses—where are you—in the sweet bye and bye—

One day I went to bed and slept for a month. (We painted the walls with a second coat.) Did you call. The color white. The difference eludes me. Not some, but all of it. (Another time) I went to sleep and never woke up again. I went to sleep and woke up. I woke up between two grains of sand. I woke up in an hour-glass. I slept between two pages of a book. I made advances toward a distant tree. I paid my respects to an ancient promise. I wished my way through an anchored storm. I ignored all warnings to turn and run. I passed out like forms in question falling downstairs. The light mimicked my stammering effort to remember. The only clarity with which we were ends

I keep thinking I am hearing someone call my name. Is it only the wind. Or the hum of the electric light bulb. Sounds of the forest, wireless messages. I want to call you, I don't know how.

Abandoned posture.

I don't believe in external circumstances anymore— go to sleep and when you wake up—you won't be there anymore—(everything will be the same).

There is no more disgust in the thought than there is in the act of the washing of another person's body than there is in the thought of or the act itself of removing one's eyeglasses to see how dirty they are and to then put them down, walking to the sink to wash them, having forgotten the necessity of bringing them to the sink to accomplish this action, then upon realizing this (knowing something was wrong, finding one's hands empty to complete a forgotten gesture, remembering then what it was that one had set out to do), looking around to find them upon which walking over to pick them up, and then returning with them to the sink to finally complete the activity.

Like a cat, catlike, the mind sits upon a shelf, itself less tense than present, more or forgetful of forgiveness, sang to one another, no one dramatic, hopeful message. Whatever gets you through the song, oh at last I've found the meaning of yearning and the longing and the full, rich, cave-shuddering sweet mystery unopened

Thank you for being so brave for having the courage to be so honest with me, I hope that I will have as much courage I shudder at the thought.

The light, extinguished, carries me home by camelback. The setting of the sun leaves much to be desired. What do you say?

Hurry to me, my sleeveless confessor bringing glad

tidings of mercy revealed within tender faults. My origin is uncertain, yet they do not confess having known me before I came here. The walk across the grass still struggling through the cold damp ground or was the mud yet soft? The earth, which clings to our feet, even as light reveals octaves, transformed like vision unimpaired.

Like a trail of breadcrumbs, bombs, resplendent bear false witness, teeth against the udder landmarks removed, you may be the only one.

Not too. If the swelling does not go down. Then what.

UNLEASHED
DEFENSES

Stuffed brains—'way out in Colorado, canoe your way into my heart yes bing bing bing little pads wouldn't it be lovely you the way when like long away unleashed defenses disguise of sheep in wolves' haunches whatever where is the post office please; do you see what I mean I meant to bring by now it would've melted dishes cornered sleep bring the flakes like tool under fear doesn't light arches wholely time wall.

The sounds through the wall—in my weakness I call to you, cloudy precautions change my mind to different resolutions, like backing up through the same distance and effort as it would take to take the long way around to the same place as is just in front of you. Seemless detour! My orientation recycles all hope of reconciliation, however, haphazardly I may proceed, as it were, as though nothing had intervened. At least, though not inappropriately, my thoughts recoiled recalling totality not decipherable as distinct within the realms of reason.

I worship you. My hand does not believe it is actually writing this. What a long body stands between a hand and its most potent desire, formed of the mind—or is it the other way around? Makes no difference, they are both the same thing. I want to hold you, enfold you and enfolded by you in our arms. Can you imagine? All it takes is a little imagination. How curious, indeed. How do we manage to do otherwise? I love you is not so clear a thought. I do not know what that means here. Rather an acknowledgement of what might be, if given the chance. But one must want to. How can I know how you feel? I know how I feel. It's always the same. But you are not. You are always you. Do you have any idea what I am feeling? If you don't, then, if you don't, then, if you did, what would you do? Should I stop thinking about it. Would you have me? The door creaks, the heat is coming up, and rattles in the pipes—the expanding of the wood, how big are you? Endless night moans, like the time we could speak no more, and could do nothing more than nothing, but perhaps we did.

Who's running this show, who's in charge here? It doesn't take much to convince yourself you ought to stay—then what happens;—well, we invented an endurance test of the way it looks when one

INSTINCT TRANSMISSION

Still the sounds, subtle—through the door, like some (strange) Morse code filtered by way of instinct transmission; I had once had ears through which to hear such throngs like tadpoles trembling in the dark

Excuse me please but may I remind you that we are both children without any names, doors which open on empty rooms, vacant houses, deserted homes, unfurnished abodes, when into which we enter, at first, fixed glance eyes upon the wall framed like dust my mirror rest in pieces up on the man tell absent tales this is what it means to fill full with broken bits be careful not so slant your wits you gnome went before the bleak break dawn I set my sights on high'r things fill dance this to n'ere be true tomb eye's elf

Take it off with both hands. With what to take it off. Tied behind your back. Any one who can not be had is not a conquest. Something is different now. The same old get-up. Get up and go, got up and went.

Give us this day our daily death and deliver us. Deal us dutifully from our nervous eating habits, save your breath for better bait.

This is the last, of this; where was it? Unmentionable explosion—no rest there is no rest there. My fingers burnt the fire. And how the window followed me home. To you, who watch, let us listen—see us through, hear our pleas. Test me always that I may sit straight as a beanpole, so may thy will be done. Teach us guide, we through the wood nocturnal, tell of the unfailing light, gentle balm of evening, sapphire of tears.

Some times I know I wonder whether everyone looks I meet on standing the corner, enough for long away gone crying, another lost name the way all night yes of but one if I think alone won't the same that you want now all right well

Why don't you just try and go to sleep

Why should I do anything? Why shouldn't I do anything. I'm trying to cover it up. But.

I can feel it working. I've been here before. I should've done a lot of things I didn't do last night. I should've done a lot of things last night. My mind is a blank. Blankity-blank my mind is white. There was no one extant as they say. Wake up there buddy go down your tube.

Listen. Less than can asbestos time tie my rewiring 'old my there is the sound of something moving within the wall effortlessly, there is still a need to breathe, deeply through the silence to the other side, which is to say the other side of what which is that which is to take sides which side of what is which. It's only something that seems less than it is are you rolling for now or to take with you when they get here oh that's right.

. . . sigh . . .   again.   The same.   Still. More or less. More than less. Who are you. Again. The same question. Without lines. Is this just passing time or passing out. Out of what. The sound of footsteps on the stairs. The final conquest. The door at the top of the stairs. Is always there. Waiting, it waits for no one.

At the end. The final light that is cast upon the face. The scene at the end. Nothing is ever the same as everything is the same. Open your eye. The time is here. Expression is ultimately received within its opposite. The obvious is clear as existing within the obscure. The reason is finally defined through the impossibility of expression of itself through any terms larger or smaller than life itself. The very fact of possibility precludes the existence of cognitive recognition.

But then, in the end, there is no explanation. The mirror is shattered, the eye is revealed.

THE INSEPARABLE CONVALESCENCE (OBLIQUE REFERENCE)

The experience of a sound forgotten, now heard like a passing cloud passing by, already obsolete, while all the while, in the other room a cat plays ball with some neglected object, his collar waylaid, strangely having taken on a life of its own. The sound now stopped, an interfering hand, another commences to begin its continuation, the occasional tap and constant gurgle, (like) a friend you'd always meant to contact, to get in touch with the difference between a metaphor and a simile the familiar sound of the heat in the pipes, comforting in bed at night, even though pajamas cling bringing a certain peace of mind and body, still there is something in the room next door the whistle of an approaching train the sudden invasion of the midnight air and returning again the quiet hum of evening the hiss of the pipes.

Again, and again, the inseparable convalescence. No trophies here—for this. All you have only to show is the look upon your face when it's over. There is not this ever present need to delete a letter, or forget the principle of rewards and bondages. The desire to defile oneself. What does this mean? Certainly one does not seek self-destruction, and let there be no mistake— when the show is over, everyone goes home.

Well, I'll tell you, six and two is eight and, uh—well; I don't know. But you have a look of surprise on your face—6 . . .   12 . . .   18 . . . ? What's it to you? Correction please, do you notice any difference in me? Well, that question mark does do something for you. It has a reputation, you know. One should be careful with such things, after all, the family image and what.

The silent teas wreak emulsions fast—the whole day is shot to hell. Send me some samples of your work. Tell me about it some other time. Right now I'm not home to anyone, not even myself. You open the door, then close it again what am I to think? Then sounds of a coat being put on, boots, and a knife slashing through cardboard—enough of your colorful words, I don't want them, thank you . . .

If I could only see through to the other side—sounds once revealed the way they are, unexpected,

You are somewhere, I can see you somewhere among the angels in a fountain, you curly hair dew-speckled, roses in your ears, your teeth of pearls, no need for speech here, cast your glance, eye of sapphire, your toenails blush at the infrared haloes, so sudden, the

unexpected watchful gaze of an unknown admirer—
(parenthetically, we are all angels, watching each
other from within our common heaven, the ground
unearthed), celestial spirits, beings of rapturous
moments, infinite bargains struck forth from within the
tomb—out of bounds we walk through forests of golden
nimbus, crowds astound us, daffodils and jonquils
rest in the embrace of spring's gentle breath; twilight
gleams in patterns unduplicable as foreign dust made
tangible, you're going away, new vistas re-arrange your
eyes before the very sight of themselves, hunger, thirst
unquenched, ever-mistrusted vigil through which my
arms arrest each other, the new-known hearts of the
lowliest branches clear our hindrance, knot bewiled my
footing, stroke these often slayed misgivings; bring new
words and worlds through which to sleep my main-
lined dreams, too weary now for life's sweet whistle, let
me see, oh solemn potion, test my veins, sweet valves
of voices, crush mine height, forget my load, my spiney,
fog-eaten lord, forgive us once more, that we begin this
time, again, as though there had been none before, thy
will be done.

There in the next room, the world waits for no one.

Nothing seems bigger than it really is. If it weren't for the loose ends hanging around the house there'd be no need for all this confusion. (Read) a book a day keeps the doctor away. Teach an old dog new tricks, will you? Well you may be in for a big surprise; if you don't watch out we may take away your ears and replace them with cancelled checks. Now there's nothing to be afraid of; merely an oblique reference to obsolete condolences in spite of the snow. Your remind me of my youth. Never eat too much and if you do remember Christmas Humphries.

You know what I mean? Watch out for fallout, but don't worry. About it. If it comes, let it. There is nothing between you and it besides you and it. And what's-his-name. Ethan Allan? Is that a sentence?

Somebody tore most of the next page off. It must have been me. It's only twelve o'clock and I am in bed already for bed. My eyelids are closing me. Were we really there at the same time? Maybe that's where I remember you from. Whatever happened that night is not worth reminiscing about. Pain in the leg. Fallout shelter. The Frank Lloyd Wright house is

Perhaps the question at this point is not necessarily

to try to play together to play together—that is can one (or two) succeed by trying? Also, the point should be clearly made that it is also as unnecessary to try to not play together to play together. This would seem to imply a necessity for a re-evaluation of intentions—why must there always be this futile effort toward which so much effort is spent and through which so little is achieved, if ever that much. The thing is to not try to inflict one's effort upon anyone as either a contradiction or an agreement.

Nothing could ever begin to express my feelings—feelings, such things as, what are they, or being so, what of it? Haven't we enough trouble without it. Robbers of thought, like a thief in the night.

Four minutes left. Nothing to say. Thinking of how much time could be spent toward that effort, saying nothing. You clear you throat. And again. What is the reason of clearing your throat when you are not going to speak? Perhaps it makes it easier to breathe. We all know what we mean when we say speak, but do we know what we mean when we say breathe? One minute late, or is that one minute early? In a hurry to catch a plane, can you take me there? I have to, I must; I have no choice. Someone sneezes. Again, another minute; a cough. Through the looking-glass wall. The light is still on; a yawn. The watch lost on the rocks. Sudden total loss of consciousness. (Memory)

Time, isn't it that settles all oases, ties most shoelaces, loosens usual schedules, for all of this time, what time is it, and what do we mean by now? Wouldn't one tire, after great length, of the feeble attempt at explanation of the act of explanation itself. Almost time to get up. Better go to sleep.

Again, this. Forget it.

It's true, I have no sense of the change
    of season.
    Good-night.

When all there has been is what there has been then what has there been. Ring bell ring. When there is nothing to know and they know nothing, then the good-doers go home. When what has been done has been done, then what has been done. Why has this been so. As the case may be, there is no way of knowing beforehand.

When it is time to give up, what time is it. When it is time to give up, what is it. When it is given, what is up. When it is up, what is up. When it is over, what is up. What is up. What is over. What is through the beading dog and under the turned order and over and through the similar consistency. We hold no claim to fame. We are but the responsibility for which there is not attendance; in former terms, the numbers of our breath dissuade us. This time there is no disturbance. We are at least as good as we look. There is no getting around the fact of the Madonna of the porch. Watchful donor of late defiled worns. Cast ties the inch betweener for thy order sake. Deft pilfer toad describer of canvas, deal swift blows. Of an armor that describes no labial torches, send all terms back late mortar fill to stave. Lend some tinder. Bell and able. Tow an

A NOVEL ABOUT SOMEONE IN THE ROOM NEXT DOOR WHOM I CAN HEAR THROUGH THE WALL

Someone came out of the wall; there was a long pause—he had eaten too much, and then went back in.

This was not the first time we had seen him. It had, in fact become a rather regular occurrence, of an evening, while in the midst of various preoccupations, to suddenly find him there among us, as though nothing could have been more commonplace.

I looked up from my knitting, when upon clearing his throat (his way of discreetly making his presence known) he proceeded to light his pipe, and began to read the evening paper.

Well, there was nothing unusual about this, except that I noticed a peculiar tension about his eyebrows (and forehead).

Was he uncomfortable among us? (We had made every possible effort to accommodate him as though he were one of the family.) Perhaps we didn't give him enough attention; but then no one wanted to make our unusual visitor self-conscious.

Was the room stuffy, or was there a draft? Did he dislike the flowers, or the song on the Victrola? I got up to offer some sherry: our friend said he preferred cognac.

I poured it, and he graciously received the glass. I could tell by the way he downed his drink that something was wrong.

He politely excused himself and quickly vanished from sight, as suddenly as he had appeared. We looked at each other with slight amusement to lift the air of bewilderment that had settled upon the room; this had happened before. I returned to my knitting.

The following evening, while clearing the dishes after dinner, I felt a peculiar sensation in my throat. Going into the kitchen to get a glass of water, I found the faucet already on; and in the previously empty sink, a goblet just full to the brim.

I turned the water off, and lifted the glass. Hesitating for a moment, before bringing it to my lips, I paused; reflecting momentarily upon the curious coincidence of the unusual events which had proliferated during the previous few weeks. Amazed by my own lack of comprehension, which had so often in the past been able to discern a cohesive pattern within the most seemingly unrelated events.

Suddenly roused from my reverie by the sensation of water dripping down my arm; ah yes, what has one to fear, in such a world as this: wherein the most extraordinary of circumstances are still bound safe within the comforting predictability of the most commonplace of earthly rules.

The warmth of the house, so secure; nothing could ever disrupt this. The calm stillness of the air, undisturbed for centuries within these walls. The depth of grain within the wood which panels these rooms; the richness of hue within the colors that filter through the leaded glass, casting a watchful eye upon our lives within these realms: ever aware, though rarely met, face to face, with that source outside ourselves, beyond these lives, from whence all things came thus to be, and by constant faith in which they are sustained.

A cup of tea, the warming sureness of this life of ours; so simple are these things which through ways complex are thereby revealed. Lemon, sugar and cream; little cakes and sandwiches. Nuts and fruit. Biscuits and muffins. Marmalade and jam. Such lovely dreaming things.

Through a wall, in the next room, someone sits. Occasionally one can hear him move. Now and again you could almost see him, there with a mushroom in his hand. He makes a sound with his throat, like a bird. One knows he is there, yet there is a constant awareness of total mutual inaccessibility. There are some things which, once acknowledged, can provide in their very irrevocability, a highly stimulating source of motivation.

There are few things in life to which one may look, as a constant, unyielding reminder of the fundamental perfection. There are few things in this world that are absolute, true and invariably reliable. They are these things, against which all else must be measured. This is the only true justice. The very existence of all that we hold most dear. Gazing out the window, I wonder how long this will last.

My truest confession is to be waiting in bed for someone to come through the door. Humming in the next room. The sound of a car going by out the window. The heat coming up through the pipes. The cat sleeping next to me. The clearing of a throat. The turning of a page. The breaking of a chain. No mail. Another page.

The sudden invasion of the evening air in the form of a late night train going by, interrupts all around itself, plowing a path through the stillness of the atmosphere contained within this little town.

The walls have ears. Lying in bed this evening, I find myself at a loss for words.

A yawn from the next room is heard through the door between us; it is him.

THE
EXTERMINATOR
OF WORDS

Returning to this room, I am in a different space. The three days which have come between us have so altered the state of things in the world. Worlds collide; there is this constant urge to thrust outward, through the crust, so long formed through the stuff of which dreams, the stuff of which throats seek forward fulfillment through the most immediate means available.

The pomegranate seed; mention the word and I remember a long forgotten embarrassment, overlooked in fifteen minutes, you have to be careful, babbling birdie by the brook, I am ashamed to have you see me like this—don't worry, I'm not seeing you, I'm just keeping house, this will be a slight thunder and then I'll rest my feet on the table, thank you kindly. Spirals defeat common designpearance.

The Bois de Boulogne
. . . in a manner of speaking.

Come across, he said. They are there.
Seen three. This is not a mistake.
Miss Hap. Tell me true.

This is how they looked. What were they looking at. A mystery. Foul play. There is something mysterious at work here. I began writing a novel. On whose account. I could not write fast enough. And still stop for punctuation. It is so tiresome. And yet one feels a sense of obligation. To elaborate. Almost as though each sentence could be a paragraph. And a complete thought is no less than an entire book. I pay my respects. I wish to pay my respects. There are so many ways of saying the same thing. One wants to say them all. One feels the necessity to say them all. But there is so much else to say. The Exterminator of Words. Shake the tree. The apples fall. Put them in a basket and take them home. This could go on forever. If we are careful. There is enough to go around. Sit down. Please.

I am a very well disciplined writer. I am a very undisciplined writer. I am not a very well disciplined writer.

I am writing a novel about someone in the room next door whom I can hear through the wall. I am writing a novel about what it would be like to hear someone through the wall in the room next door. I am writing a novel about what it would be like to be writing a novel about someone in the room next door whom I can hear through the wall. I am making believe that there is someone in the room next door whom I can hear through the wall. I am making believe that I am writing a novel about someone in the room next door whom I can hear through the wall.

To write a novel about someone in the next room one must be in the room to which the other room is next. Having removed oneself momentarily from said room, there is no going back. That is to say that when one does return, nothing is the same, everything is changed, everything is different.

There is no longer someone in the room next door, I am the one in the room next door who is no longer there. As long as I am no longer there, there is no one there. For all practical purposes, let it be said that there never was anyone there. As long as I was there, there was no one there.

There are voices through the walls; the walls not only have ears, they have mouths. They speak in tongues, saying what they feel, not what they mean.

Standing by the roadside, a man passed me, jogging

along; he passed two or three times around, in the course of his path. Finally he stopped, and said hello. We spoke a while, and he invited me to have a drink with him at the pub we were standing by. I found out later, that he was the proprietor of the place.

Returning to the room we fell upon ourselves, wrestling with each other, like so many angels in the dust; we devoured our flesh, and ground our souls, half-starved, as in the midst of the desert.

Teething on our bones, we fled the realms of conscious fact, gluing our thoughts toward patterns formed of outwardly contradictory seizures.

Looking toward one another we received guests whose presence though oblique, already wandered through our eyes, passing freely hither and yon, like boys in flight from thieves who come to steal not what they know, but possess those apples hung ripe upon the tree of their own fruition.

Friction between the palms increased our willingness to overcome any abandonment of morals we might have retained as a remnant of former categories, the bondage of which we had long since transcended.

The however intergalactic spewings which spurned our kingdom's mouth, henceforth uttered no longer tracts through its own self-contradictions, that any ability to utter forth a similarly benign transformer at the point of seduction, would have so utterly permeated our entire conception of the continuity we had against all obstacles achieved, as to threaten our fundament where it lives most deeply seeded to the core of its foundation, that the merest scratching at the door, as it were, of temptations such as we were at the time so overtly susceptible to, could have easily gone past our perineum quicker than a bolt of lightning and more jagged though, upon its removal than an umbrella turned as the proverbial inside-out.

Having no way out, we succumbed willingly, to the drastic measures of our gargantuan entanglement, which proved sublimely acute, and left us quivering in the quickly melting snare of our own undoing; sucked through, within the precious fluids of the rarest of sources, extracted meticulously through fine siphons, tubes which might bring remedy to the most copious of origins.

The fear that this feeling, of such pure intent, might

by very recognition of itself become corrupt, halts its progress, stunts coming of age and stops dead in its tracks.

This fear, so profound, might serve in fact to stifle all potential for growth, ultimately leads one to find other channels as outlets to let out this feeling of futility, through which one proceeds through most of life.

Turning off the light before closing one's eyes like a glacier moving toward the ocean; one floats downstream to melt at last, within the one water to which all things must course: that of all things which is the source.

With this, with this; now that it's here, I come to greet you time and again. You know who I am before I knock: the door is closed. I arrive after hours, or before opening, at closing time; the coast is clear. Not so much as a sound is heard; I enter without knocking. The stillness is shattered; on the way home, we stop to replenish our energy; I'll owe it to you if that's alright. You know where you can find me; I knock without entering. I've waited this long, I might as well continue; Looking through a window I remember walking down a village street and something in a window: you are sitting inside me for which I am very grateful; we shall always each know where the other is and all else failing, we'll meet again back home.

This is the secret: I am here and I am not here. I do not know where I am. I know less and less each minute; striving for a spontaneity that becomes ultimately the ongoing moment itself, I often pass ahead of time, thereby getting nowhere slowly. I do not know who I am so I certainly don't know you. On the other hand, I do not know myself, therefore I could not know you.

GRIM MOTORS
THE VACANT
MOMENT
SURRENDERS ITSELF
TO THE PENETRATORS
OF VULNERABILITY

Now, at night, I lie here and listen to the vacant sounds that come through the air to my ear; grim motors that leap through foreign substance, vagrants who question without having ever been asked—I want to know if what they are trying to say can tell me something about you, something I want to know, which they do not know I want to know. I must make them tell me without it being apparent that I am the least bit interested—it is only in this way, that I may ever know who you are.

They begin to speak; I listen attentively in anticipation of each breath, an awakening syllable. Roses grow from their ears in place of headphones, and without my noticing it. Somewhere someone has just picked up a phonograph needle which had been skipping for some time and has lifted it off the record; a slight moan was heard as soon as this occurred. It was as though someone had remembered something they had forgotten long ago, and lost all hope of remembering, thereupon, much later, at long last recollected, at the point at which all consciousness of any effort whatsoever had passed—the vacant moment surrenders itself to the penetrators of vulnerability.

In the meantime, countless feathers fall from my head. Instead of stuffing olives as an indication of questionable destiny, our motives were clearly defined this time and readily observable as the growths which grew upon the masks in which we hid, behind them, took root within our countenance; leaving no trace above the surface in which these grounded their airs, none bore witness against the grain toward whose meandering lineage, Fate, lugubrious counsellor, the piercing sound of whose arrival sliced the air of morning even as slowly down this cheek from eyes above a tear wends its way, descending like a diamond cutting glass.

In the process of turning inward the movement through the passage which in the past has pushed out toward the other side might also every other thing respond in like movement the removal of the outward imperative would seem to also remove many corresponding analogues in the light of day or behind closed doors.

The completion of a thought might become a complex process greatly impeded by such enforcements. There would seem to result a change in direction of whether or not was drawn toward watered whistle or down to watered what.

Many have resolved to play their lives out the best they know how, and wait for the end to come.

I AM SITTING IN A CHAIR BY A WINDOW IN A ROOM AND THE AIR IS STILL

So now how where are who and you going have we met? Yet, yes; you know this slows down the process, slight clicks emerge, once more inside the storehouse of the imagination, the holes in the sheets—hopeless: occasional taps like heartbeats—tap; diverse and sundry items for audibility—slow down, you hear? Listen— close your eyes, you'll see (!) that you hear better that (this) way. Do you hear what I mean? Are you here/not here? Do you read me. I can read you like a book. Like an open book. What are you doing tonight—the war is over, they have ordered unconditional surrender— there is nowhere to go to surrender!

We have not surrendered—we pull out just in time to let them surrender. You must excuse us, but we would/could not have borne the pain.

Something about the skin of our teeth, was it? Eh? . . . Well, it's just as well; if you asked me, the whole thing's a bloody nuisance which we could do well without. It's like some—from 'way back somewhere, it keeps on slipping out, you know, like something you thought you'd forgotten about, pull it out of your mind; and there it was all along, just waiting for a chance to slip out again.

Sitting alone by the window (I know what I mean), I see the air, it moves: I am still, sitting alone by the window, and the air is still. In the room where I am sitting, the air is still; I am sitting in a chair, by a window in this room, and the air is still. It is quiet here; I can see the air moving outside. I am sitting in a chair by a window in a room; it is quiet outside. The air is still; in the room I am sitting in, I can see the air move. I am sitting in a chair in a room by the window; outside, it is quiet. I can see the air moving. Alone, in a room, I sit in a chair by the window; the air is still. It is quiet here; outside the window, I can see the air moving. I am sitting in a room, outside the window; I am alone, and the air is still. It is quiet, and in the window, I can see the air moving. I am alone; sitting inside a window, the air is still. Looking outside, I can see the air moving; it is quiet, and I can see the chair. I am alone; I am sitting outside the window. It is cold; and in this way, my hands press against the glass. Through the chair, I can see the air moving; it is quiet, and I am still inside the room.

Pressing my eyes inside my hands, I see the chair, lying on its back; the air is clear, and I am still sitting on the window. Looking through the air, I see the room. Closing my eyes, I can hear the air move; it is quiet, and the window is not open. In the room, I am sitting in a chair; it is dark, and I can nearly see my hand in front of my eyes. The window is closed, and outside I can hear the sound of trees moving in air. It is quiet, and my eyes press out against my cheeks. Inside the window, I can hear someone moving a chair around the room. I closed my ears, and looked out the window; it was dark outside, and the light was on in the room. Through the air, I could see someone I know. The chair collapsed; we cannot sit in it anymore. It is quiet, and outside the window I can see the air moving.

Don't stop. I am sitting up in bed. I hear him through the door, asleep in the next room, snoring. Settle down; listen. Too many, not enough things. No, not nearly enough of anything; perhaps it always seems that way. A slow boat to Greenland; we arrive at dawn. Suddenly, on dry land—a ladybug falls on my head; there is a difference between where we are and what it might have been like if I hadn't gone away. My eyes are trying to close on me—why do I resist?

Give me an idea; maybe this has nothing to do with ideas, the realm of substance—do you follow? How can I explain? What happens when things change; obviously and influentially.

All the fingers point the same way: that way. It doesn't always work. You came to see me, you left. That night under the streetlamp; a night much like this one, a night much like our own. A life much like our own. You know, that could mean almost anything; you should've been there. Maybe you were; I couldn't see, what with the umbrellas and all. It was as though we were all afflicted by that same disease: dis-ease. This ease I felt was quite peculiar, considering the time of year and all; it had not, in the past, been at all an unusual thing for me to summon to my side, what was then remaining of my scattered faculties, the greater part of which, were on leave of absence; having taken leave of my senses, momentarily I paused and reflected upon the various and diverse attempts that had been made in the past in circumstances not unlike my own, by persons of greater presence than I, striving toward the clarity of unafflicted sight, the vision of which held treasures far beyond any concept formed in desperation as facsimiles to the true and veritable source from which all illumination pours, and to which, exhausted, the weary return. The regenerative properties of such a well of potential might serve to sufficiently intrigue our interests as to discourage any

ACTUAL BREATH CUTS DOCILE EVOLUTION THE POSSIBILITY OF SUCCESSFUL INTERACTION AMONG THOSE INVOLVED

attempt whatsoever to attain beyond that which has been given, and through no unnatural devices to devise a moment of comprehension of the most intangible of causes and their consequent effects, which might prove advantageous to all concerned. Of course, there were to be difficulties; and of the sort, I might add, that dissuade interference with the affecting at once of certain measures of desperation, brought into play as reasonable rationalizations within an extremely complex framework toward which we move, slowly, and continue until we have come 'round a full circle, at which point one might as well peel potatoes, what for the unfed mouths clucking for their meat-- "That's the one I want!"

I am so glad I was wearing my shoes. The sudden unexpectedness of lack of solitude. She came too; I must not forget their list, corrections included. I am not certain of what this means, nor am I correct in assuming an unrequested posture, for which I have given no explanation, with or without anyone's consent.

Edible fog—(a procreative fact?)
FROZEN THRILLS

He was aware of the fact. He was aware of the fact that he was aware. He was aware of the fact that he was aware of. He was aware of that. He was aware of that fact. Of that he was aware. Of that fact he was aware. That he was aware of that fact was no accident.

Of that he was quite aware. In fact, he was quite aware of the fact of which he was aware. Aware of that, of that fact, he was where he thought he was. He was there, where he thought he was; in fact, this was not an accident, either.

Either he was there (where he thought he was), or else he was there (where he thought he wasn't). There he was, exactly where he thought he was, exactly where his thought was; but was he—really was he there, actually there; in fact and in intention, was he actually there, in intention there, factually there in intention actually, there intentionally there, in actuality there, infractionably there, without and within, fully there?

There was a way; where there is a will there is a way. There where there is will there is a way. Where there is will there, there is a way. There where there is will, there is there way. Where, where is their will, there

there is their way. There, where there is their well, there is their whey. Weigh their will against their whey. Will there their will, well against their ineptitude. Rest their wheel against their wall, relax their wind while there is wool. Wend their whey away; win their war aweigh! Winter thy wilted west, when there were numerous whethers. Wheel my form aghast that cog from whence new wonders will! When you take weather and watch our stencils, staple their invention while we wart whistles. Station those calibrators, to fill their holy mutants; whisk all turning futures toward the word which wound its way upon the eave. Torn to torment final e's for their own massive seeds. Test every fodder for pressing blades of auction. Full through to the other most insipid diesel dormer, tool the break from veil a sedentary gill.

Strong the mutinous avarice from whence thy former blood coons dent every fresh herd igneous jewel keys lest Mormon news open pressing queers run storming tender uvulas varicose wench Xavier yawned zeal.

Actual breath cuts docile evolution from growth hogs inside June kissed lemurs many none order personal quintuplets rather stately turned under very wordy x-its yours.

There is no expectation. There are no exceptions to the rules. If. I knew what I was going to say would I have said it. Do you know. To say what is clear as plain as day—is the easy way—No! It is the hard way. There is no easy way.

The name of being night. Like red ink, traditionally capitalized and punctuated like an unexpected ride from the proscenium to entire repatriated gestures on the contrary.

They left. The place they had lived in was now occupied by someone else. Occupied by someone else. This was not a hindrance, nor were there any regrets as to the current plan for the following year.

All rights had been reserved and when they moved away, although they leaned admirably forward, their backs would tend to tell them otherwise.

What was required of them at this point in no way removed any sense of responsibility, intentionally from their shoulders.

Any confusion which resulted from the overfeeding of the population at large, lessened considerably the possibility of successful interaction among those involved.

Like attracts like, so they say.

The light bulb was a constant reminder.

This is the one—this is the one that must be used. The others can be put aside. This goes beyond what it had been thought to be. At least. There is no merit to be attached to it. The gesture is in itself complete. A perfection of coincidence. Perhaps you'd be sorry. Even though you knew the consequences. There was nothing to stop you from putting an end to it. Maybe I'm getting too close for comfort? What is this overwhelming weight within the eyes?

Wait and open. And do not open. Put the socks on and lay your head down on the pillow. Tell me what you dreamed to-day. Isn't that nice?! Cut it open—yes; open the envelope and let me see what it is. It's a letter for me. Open it—not without the difference in our way.

Soon, soon.

Soon, soon. Pressed lips—too tight. Discomfort is only the beginning. The initial initiation. Don't waste time. Don't be afraid of wasting time—it can not be wasted. Nothing is wasted unless you don't use it.

I bought myself a new pair of shoes with a sense of apprehension. Happy landing. You could hear the sound of the highway from it. Deliberately indecipherable. The screen is so blurry I can barely see it. Remember me? Punctuation marks. I think I'm going to be getting involved with them. A simple statement. And I just made the bed, too. To keep it warm until I am ready for it. Cultivating mushrooms. Cutlery. Close the door. Go ahead, why don't you, and run around the room? Stuffed to the gills. I would just love that little brick house in town. You'd better go up now and put that all away. Do you think you could really tear yourself away from this now? I really had not considered any other possibilities. I'll think about it. Someone we both know and it's not you. You're going to turn into an icicle. Thank you for the blueberries. Let's go into another room; everyone else has heard it already. Today was the first time I picked it up since I have been here. 58 cents each. It was no fault of mine. I certainly will never do that thing now. Gentle receptor. Open my blessings. You should meet her. Hear the quiet strains.

There. There are. There are people. There are people living. There are people living at the end. There are people living at the end of the world.

There are people living at the end of the world where there is no sun. Where the sun can not come through. The light does not penetrate.

Where the clouds are thick. Where the clouds are so dense. The light can not shine through them. Cannot pass through.

The sky is translucent. Like a shoji screen. The light is not blue. Vision objective? Strained through the tea. Prayers. Willingly granted. Like the sound of it. Inherently ambiguous. Which do you like better?

So many ways. Saying same the turn, the thread; opened. Said the distant hum. Go on. A pressing need. Dispense with articles. I would rather change. Remembering portrait. Distinguishing characteristics. No cause for. Hold. Pound into. It said. Split rocks. This mean? Absolute non. Describe please. Remove tension. Eyes. To go.

It. Haven't taken me an hour. To pour the tea. Afterwards finally spilling it. Makes me wonder. Whether or not. I really belong. Here.

Far too long, have the ashes smouldered, the ashes of unrequited love; unstirred, yet not yet cold—the heart murmers still: a faint drum beat across the field of time's inconstancy; static syncopation of memories, needful of water; gentle balm of recognition—the light of the eye extending beyond its field of vision.

Attic-dust. Thick within. The arms of secrecy. Disturb no thoughts. Tip-toe silent. His good sleep. Clothed my eyes.

A window. Or rather a pain. Pain of dust. Poised mid-air. Stilled in flight. Brought low. Before the moth.

Another chance? Question. Mark the minutes. Come again.

Climb the stairs. The rope hangs down. What left?

Nobody's Fool. The secrecy of a stranger. No going back.

Take care. Once again.

Sounds. The way I feel.

Try again. What?

Don't say I didn't tell you.

Enough. Far too long, too many years. Stir the ashes, for me, please. You remember how we used to do it. Things were simpler, then. Easier, too.

Now, . . . there is just no consistency, no constancy. Consistently inconsistent. Constantly inconstant.

So the beavers returned to the pond. It was a

different pond. Not the pond we walked by. Somewhere else. What made them do that? A homing instinct of some kind? Who wouldn't. If only it were so simple. But it's like swimming upstream. You see.

You should never have let me stay home from school. I couldn't make it without some structure—nothing to hold to—there was nothing left. I never could tell you, so many things—now plague my memory.

The past is irrecoverable, but we are not. However, one must face up to a lot of things we'd rather sweep under the rug; they will not rest, or give me peace.

It's like running after something you can't catch up with—waiting for something that never comes. The frustration is unbearable—a feeling of intense helplessness.

We then contrive any number of means to subdue the pain—the easy ones don't work any more—liquor, grass, drugs, sex, art.

More invisible, subtle, and internal means must be employed; such that can not be found by any one, and exist without the slightest dependence on the user for any of his conscious attentions.

A means by which one may successfully (for all apparent purposes) continue one's life in the face of the most seemingly insurmountable obstacles. It is in fact through the mental negation of the very existence of these hurdles that the mind is able to relieve itself of responsibility for its own actions.

The facile illusion of attaining a state of self-focused mind, may also be maintained and successfully projected for the benefit of the belief of others, while all the while the mind is in continual state of blind focus— it knows not what it sees, nor even sees consciously any longer.

The state may be compared with that of dream, as a fluid condition in which events, people, places, things intermingle and a general feeling of well-being may even be manifest.

However, the one difference distinguishing this from its parallel in the normal waking world—is the feeling of helplessness, of distance, and of an essential non-involvement, as though the entire experience of life were passing by, as though viewed on a very grey and rainy day, through a window.

However comforting any scene may be, however

warm a passing emotion may feel, however close one may come toward a feeling of good, a sense of well-being, it is ultimately followed and

cancelled out by the most abysmal sensation of remorse.

This too, has been so long romanticized as being analogous to some state of poetic reverie, or spiritual crystallization, one may, in time come to cherish it early. It is as necessary as air, this tragic relief.

How peculiar it might seem to one who has not experienced it, never touched upon it in the farthest recesses of the imagination. But, just so peculiar does it seem, and even inconceivable, that anyone could bear the pure sensation of joy!

How unfortunate; and yet, how lucky they—who may breathe the light of day unfiltered through the darkening hands of night. How to breathe—a foreign world; brilliance unearthed—unabashed luminescence!

It is as though there was only one entire day of my life when I went for a walk. This was not the green pen period. Decidedly so. One had long made overtures toward this effect. Long since one had made known desires to put into effect efforts toward that effect; letter days read less and less than orchids, ineffectually.

Had known distinction within realms not unfamiliar inning hours door ancestors; take comma rest don't from these oceans, overt wit in their dread shingle ears purr est elong rather host full entity telegram in porcelain madrigals shoot foreign decibles straight through to the cornered heart.

When the sun went in, I brought the chair out onto the porch. A change of weather: the fields of yellow. Baggage reclaimed. Heat deterred. Burdock derailment. Sent home. No hold dimmer torn mystery enthralled; enthroned by midmorning. Station to station. No full order, clear to the point of departure.

Three pair of graphs, into the depth of honor flash the ribs on dormant tenths. Worn to be tangled forest went before or dust fair branded, you meant pour than trim ice paved crust.

Toward pressed out gulls, inter too dark onto hope far tin rooms over destined torso. Went tip born toeless fortuna wept blame ordinary duty forced bordello, yet manners paint tendrils into potion's court.

Totality pursued octagonal gifts, indifferent destruction over-rated horses fenced tightly roaming o'er dawn's tomb. Winter turned bare teeth for woolen boarders outwardly deifying film-like breath, yonder man pardoned torment intravenously patterned center.

The interior is the place from where

I don't know where, the nothing knocks. The eyes close.

However far I wander in my thoughts return to you. And this is said exactly as it is meant. Can it be true? I say to myself, "Oh no, not again"; but then I hear your voice in my ear, or see your smile in my mind's eye.

"What do people think, when they see us together?" I muse to myself.

I was just thinking: "The sun goes in when we come out."

Form-like, like form; like unto like it is it uncontrollable. To have had enough, more than enough. Something is needing being said, as simply as possible. The only clues are the ones you choose. We always wanted to go there, we went there, we have been there. By means of punctuation, in tiny sips.

On the elevated train one night, on the way home from somewhere.

To unwind. Not an easy thing to do. Yet if there is no lack of enthusiasm, there is no lack of sympathy although on the wrong side.

Once there was a fool. He had no ears. Do not disbelieve me—for he could hear many things. It is they, he said—who do not have even ears—it is they said he to himself, who say unto themselves, we must purify ourselves.

Again, he walked to the place and washed his hearing thing. This was a daily ritual with him. By doing this, he was able to reach great heights of audible insight.

The internal realms to which he attuned himself were not of his own imagination. They were actual things beyond his own experience and comprehension.

Nothing can stop me, he knew.

One day something spoke to him—he said—

It is I who speak to you—it is not you who are speaking—it is you who are listening. This is how you may know who you are—by listening to me speak— you may know that it is not you who is speaking, but rather I, and therefore it is you who is listening.

If you apply yourself to this devoutly, you may, in time gain great self-knowledge.

The fool was grateful. He applied himself devoutly to listening to the voice that spoke to him, and though he could not understand that which he said unto him, he nonetheless listened attentively and gave himself up totally to the great and profound mystery which was continuously revealed to him; though he heard not a word of it, he understood intuitively and attained considerable wisdom.

One day, as he was engaged in some menial task, another voice overcame him; at first he did not know what it was, so different was its character from the first; and then when he comprehended its nature, he began to discern its message as thus—

Behold! I am not that which you think me to be! Oh, you, who know not of any thing which is foreign to you—thou, who art so seemingly wrapt in thine own misconceptions, hear me!

For I come not in any feeble form; I carry the winds in my breath, I hold the mountains in my thought, and I move the seas with my blood.

Tell me now, do you know me as I am?

The poor fool, so unprepared for such a grand visitation, was flabbergasted, and knew not whereof he spoke, uttering thus—

Oh! Thou whisper of my trees—thoughts, can it be so? I know not, not I, no, not I know of such—not such!

Whereupon the sands were uplifted, trees uprooted—birds were overwhelmed and fell a'moulting; the seas dried up as they spoke, and the air turned to a multitude of funnels, unending unbeginning.

Trees, again peeled their thoughts like so many unutterable advantages; and lastly the form of the fool, now stripped of all its bare untidy tremblings, frail as love, stood still, as though some great and unfathomable profundity had overcome him in his very path, footsteps stilled—

Destination and departure had become one—unified, as principles beyond which there is no beyond: before which, there being none—none, none, and none being not none, nor nothing, beyond beyond beyond.

This entire book was written on inspiration.

I am deaf and dumb. Blind, my eyes can not see even in the dark without the aid of a wobbly flashlight.

And for dessert, what have we?

Someone's house just burned down. The reason given was lightning. What if I am blamed for it? I have an alibi: I was at a puppet show, at the circus. No one would believe it.

She rustles in her sheets. She is in the next room. She is across the hall. Am I here?

Crumbs on the bed. You'd never believe what I shall not say.

You have, doubtless, returned by now. This time I don't know you.

Next door is a long way.

Like turning a page, I pretend to say something. It is no use, because there is no waste of time.

No such thing, although I may return the books. Unfinished poems.

These don't grow on trees. People don't want to use their heads.

Work at it, like singing.

Uses change. So do birds

Time: it's been a long one. Since Tuesday. Until Tuesday. There is no difference. An orange blanket among the walls. The four walls. Peaches. Cream. The color of mushrooms. Nice floors. Can you just go in? Blue. Like a lamp. Something on the wall. The mirror table. Tomorrow. Chocolate. As long as there are some in the other.

Someone goes into the next room and closes the door. The door disappears into the next room and closes someone. Someone disappears into the door and closes the next room. Some room goes through someone and disappears next door.

Some door moves around a room trying to find the place on the wall through which someone is trying to walk from the other side. A doorknob stays motionless as the door turns around it trying to open itself. The room stands still as the doorknob turns around, while someone moves furniture around downstairs or next door.

I am writing about something of which I am unaware; someone with whom I am entirely unfamiliar. This, as usual, is nothing new. There'll be no distinction here, not here. Here, not here; the rabbit man.

This is not to no avail, by any means. Like the chance coincidence of the dripping of the faucet in the sink with the ticking of the clock on the refrigerator; my pen moves steadily across the page.

I can assure you, its motivations are of the purest intent. For, though I thought I stopped the water from its dripping, even now it drips. And, though I wind the clock before I go to bed, it stops of its own accord.

Yet, though I remove my pen from the paper, should I set it down again? There is no telling what it will do next. It is precisely this that is of the uttermost importance in my procedure.

When one extends oneself, into the realms of probability, one runs the inevitable risk of getting cut. Caught in the act. It is this which we are afraid of. We know all the lines, we know the ropes.

This is sticking one's neck out. Putting your head on the chopping block. No more excuses, please. Nobody wants to hear them.

Very good with lemon juice.

PART TWO

THE JOURNAL OF A PROFESSIONAL LUMP ON A BOG

And wooden sand-boxes. To sing us to sleep. Upon the 3-tiered cake. Lowered a box-spring out the attic door. Peculiar taste in the mouth. Smell in the nostrils.

A well-tuned cucumber Self-adjusting mechanism. Perhaps somewhere there is a secret box.

Dent, dent: open the gate my ailment is not so swollen. Open open! Tell me don't you seethe often around the breeze and the gate at the thorn, golden golden lies the moongold—test me—test me like darning darn darned drains remember like that time we met you said said you remembered.   Didn't you?

Oil-lined oil; oil-lined liniment: oil-lined line linen dough-often oiled extra-lined-liniment. Offering lexical lined extra length linoleum. Lentil lint lent long lovely language laboriously laughed, "Lo; land long-leaped!"

Conflicts resolved he is now embark' . . .   he is now setting settling, sold servants to the Thames, so thanks, prerogator—but the pension which you had neglected to mention appeared in the most impressive of form, not molded until the will takes over.

I am going to sit down and write; there are many things that want saying, in many different ways. Don't be a fool, and think that there are any more than the one way that you are saying this. If you said it in another way, you'd be saying something else. What needs to be said, must be said, and in the manner by which it is being expressed. Some things are necessary, others are not. Some things are as important in their "non-existence" as others are in their "existence." So many nameless deaths, they shall remain nameless, like unborn babies, still-born. The wind in the willows. A blinking light, and then the white porch. And ice-cream, coneless in the bottom on the bottom of a bag or container. Some-one's name is on it, it is black; I am talking to some-one and he is too. Again the wind, like an ocean breeze without the ocean. A seven-layer cake. Diving for sponges. Digging up roots and a broken leg. A train moves slowly, on the bottom of the sea. The Black man speaks to me, in somber tones, radiates an ancient hue, an aura of smoke and gold-dust, like a giant larva; moth to be, spinning his cocoon, as we speak, stands up by a truck that sells ice-cream. The bells are ringing. He passes on an ancient wisdom, speaking in a language extra-ordinary, yet made of the most common words. The sky is grey and darkening: his ominous message instills in me great confidence. The part I am to play, I have not memorized the lines, I write them as I go along. As far as the one who says he'd do it better, there is no way for him to take the wheel. Promise is a partridge. Passing along the road I pass my aunt, in our automobiles; we recognize each other through the windows, and travel backwards for a great distance to regain each other. We have changed, indeed, she says I look unwell, and as I tell her of my new life in the theatre, she proudly points out my cousin and his girl-friend (full-grown) and playing or working in the dirt at the side of the road with toy shovels and pails, they are busy moving it from one place to another, and then back again.

On, back to the theatre, where the elderly Negro ice-cream man has put a scoop on the bottom of the bag or container, it is nearly black, licorice or some other flavor; I'd also asked for peach-almond or something but it would not come out of the scoop. On the stage, we perform a very existentialist play; two people, I, a man and another, a woman. We are sitting at a table reading newspaper and sewing. Somehow that table has an awful lot to say; the table is like a pet dog, house-broken, he is part of the family. This play could go on for-ever.

Tell tall Toledo (Spain). You have in-deed gone along your way. Bunches in the dead-ringers. Fall among the apes. Danger before trees. Duty unbound along trains. Disasters held breath beyond the sea. Of wings and then removed not once again. Song, indeed turned over. Devastation unknown. Portly prince of calls. Sights up from the front. Sit upon the drain. Come back, I don't know where to, but come.

Now I am going to tell you about it. I hadn't wanted to bring it up, but now that you mention it, it is really most extraordinary.

"Turn back," he said. "There is another towel." They locked the door, and stealthily removed all visible signs of activity from the scene itself. Worn dimensions, within the forms of egrets. Salient sighs remove torn dressings from the ventriloquist's labia major. Deliquescing, demurely, we proceeded to give back our foundry. Intentions move in sullen weights. Wishful, wistful, like harmony, at all; he wants to outdo himself.

Here is to whom; and the clarity is not as it has been or may, shall we say, be distinguished by incongruous characteristics. There is a change afoot; great changes are afoot. Pancakes: she was raised on the thin ones—crepes; crepe souls, suzette. The thick ones in the mist, in the midst of them—it makes her want to pour maple syrup or something on them. Hems them up. They seem to need it. Not the same as what was what's-his-name was, ywis. Taken in, at the seems; the clicking that has come to be known as one of his sounds, in the making. In the making; so what was it that was what it was with you? Know what? It's true. A cup of clothes, won't you? Stay awhile. She sounds just like an hourglass, the slow drip, of a drop in the bucket. It's you I want to write about. Not write around. You astound me, once again. I am as equally amazed by our not making love now as I was by our making love before. After many turns around the block I stopped the cab and went into the Smiler's to get a roast beef on rye. There's something in my eye and it's you. I do not want to try to impress you. I want to impress you. I want desperately to impress you. I have dreams, I do not discard them. They make me remember my waking state; and reality.

And all that jazz. A vow against stealing. Anything. What does that mean. A feeling of rejection. But you sound so nice when you say it. My hand cannot keep up with my thoughts. To translate them into verbal terms, linguistic transformation of thought patterns, essentially pure; what is pure? I love your red hair and freckles. You must be doing something right, right? Right now the only right is write. And write. Bent over one's work. All night.

"4 Eggs: or was it 6?"

The tree moves, and listens;

"Do you know," he added, "that, considering the time of year, not failing to regard the season," he mused on, "and not neglecting to note the hour," he continued, "it is not without a certain unrest, that one might observe several occasionally typical occurances, well contained within the realm of probability, and yet not quite without an unusually hearty dose of the extraordinary . . . "

A hush came over the crowd which had so suddenly assembled at the scene of this soliloquy, which we have just witnessed. The Czar took particular notice of this unexpected quiet.

Motioning briefly, though explicitly to the attendant at large, forty elephants were let loose upon the field of the arena to the amazement of those assembled.

Is like to lake as land in image. An image is torn as nature; born of the hive-run stature; looks stately at the brooks, and emerge like as a thorn of late unto his hand—to emerge as one with her natural tendencies; which he found to be read as a book, and eminently readable; lend it out she said to herself, without a moment's hesitation; no decision was required.

The lake looked apart from itself; askance, as it were, as it was the time to dance: Lifted hoof and horn in time to prance upon the edging of the shore-line, densely foot bowed down upon foot—legibly to excess—the intermittent instance grasped hold of by the ankles; with both hands astride the strand, well held houses fell not down unto the ground, yet leapt, simultaneous, into the new green brink of air, upon the wayside, down among the hillocks, found one's new lost ways, long emerging chains without the graying of their customary glasses, next to kindred nest of kind red souls, souls upon the feet of mentioned sadness;

men shunned sadness; long before the winds that mock repeating glands bear witness, forced as yet, another turn of phrase, perhaps, long-linked through miles of many motioned thrills since passed, like the sound—too soon, of all the constant eagles in their tents, flown away, not long for other certain kills, we learn to doubt, no doubt, by our mistakes, and yet we make amends, though long put-off descriptions stand in envy. New envoy and The Lady of The Lake stands poised, and thrilling, sobbing at the sands and beating at the gills.

Moist clefts lean back against her shoulders, gasp upon the wounds fair-wound, drawn up athwart the staring mouths of autumnal inference, counters space; alive as fish as birds in space, replenished eye lids crave a trace of ecstasy among the leaves of grace. Long meadows blow sweet hair amast their ears to hear the songs of chills and strings the whole night long.

There was something far from wrong, and yet the stage was set, for nothing right or wrong. My eyes encircle sacred pools in secret, cools and frowns cold.

The stage is set among the new-sewn violets in warmth of primrose bath of sky-light filled with rainbow dust and particles of air-wings' breath. Note from atomizer to philodendron pharmaceutical intentions, nothing is left of heat. It is not the same anymore. You have known what was meant by these things, after all has been said and remembered, what much more is there left to remember and besides what is left?

Bend the gold of your golden thoughts into gold of your golden thoughts! Keep on, keep going, don't wait, don't waste a minute—keep the heat, the heat which is within your own mind and soul, mind and body, body and soul. Don't let up—don't lose it—don't lose it for a minute—all is lost when you lose it—keep it hidden— in the corners of the inside of your mouth way back in the lining of your cheeks.

PLEASE DON'T TELL TO JOSEPH CORNELL:

Larkspur, wrinkles . . . belt and atrophy; the distance purges this, this time as always. Think distinction's wish fulfilled, a prophecy in indigo ink and wood. Wells wished warm Dover winters any way you slice it . . . nothing removes itself from density: always this density, intermingles. Individuals apprehend consciousness in a moment's notice. A novice in moonlight dotes upon the werewolves of inactivity. Startling, lemonade and crinkle-cut tentacles form bleary-eyed instincts across immobile plateaus where wavering vestibules send darts of honeyed filaments, testing their fragrancy, Denver excluded. "Please don't," an utterance from abroad the cavernous ceiling where we walked as though unaware of where we were.

In heaven, certain centuries removed themselves in order of the next of kin from whom no man returns. That which placeth luck between the sieve of time began no mere entanglement among lean unsure connectives, that had broken terse remorse.

Nine cats, which in between the moon and "watch-out-for-them" 's crossed severally, insistent nonetheless by their still instincts, long transgressed; they delved into their cornerstones, unalarmed as though minor thoughts had ceased existing in the endless journey forward.

Dead ears, strung about the chains upon the chairs as warning to all who dared come near, to linger briefly, in fact to dare not enter further than their minds' cold habitat might permit them access. To the other world take leave—and give no signs or signals with the hand of unsupposed views without which whom might know not wherewithal to greet those stone-age kinsmen, whose ill ship marked death, uncertain for star-borne monumental grips. To leave their silken moments where they found them, meant much difficulty, left arraigning their dispersals, all in all in all in all outlived for what they were; it is not all, is it not all there is before us and as well as not around us where we lie into our selves without our shirts unbuttoned skirts fly open at the all-embracing thought of it as though we would not mind.

Our swift and deft discussions lead us home at every point unknown yet wistful like the evening humor that pervades the open mind.

EACH
MAN
HIS OWN
MONSTER

Each man carries within himself his own personal monster made in his own image (of and by his maker) of his own undoing. This absolute monstrosity abides within (which seeks its own abode at favored birth of the other), sits quietly by waiting, hoping for a chance to hop out and make its pre-sense known.

This personal monster, evolved through equanimity, displays no outward signs, but needs must incline himself toward expression of a more inward nature. He is involved, as it were, within the brief confines of the discretest to effect a subtle mastery of the structure which most immediately surrounds it, daring not for a minute to expose itself, by outward movement, which is not within its scope of possibilities, at any rate.

He remains, rather, confined within this context in which he finds himself. He looks out onto a world which he knows only through the eyes of the one within whose form he is entombed. He hears the sounds of another realm which he may only listen to. His mouth opens on to the lips of him within whose mouth he lies, listless; his tongue contained within the other's tongue, his teeth encased within those others; his voice lies, restless within vocal chords which stir themselves to a tune that has no words.

His feet, wanting to move, remain immobile, and their toes, which itch to squirm and wiggle, writhe like worms, in another's feet, like shoes laced up too tight, the things contained therein, wrestle within them, sweating and swearing under their breath.

The hands, frantic, contained, as it were, within gloves which one cannot remove, having taken on a life of their own, enforcing movements, foreign to the one within, committing acts the other never would.

The arms which thrash about to no avail, make scarcely even motions to the effect of which their intentions prompt them, in no way executing their own true goals, hidden as they are within the sleeves of another's coat, as scarves are sometimes stuffed to be put out of the way, when a coat is hung up.

The legs that bend unceasingly to run or jump and leap, to no success, the thighs constrict, the calves stretched taut, the knees are held at bay; the mechanism poised, in short, to plunge, is stayed in the effect of its efforts.

This trunk; this body; packed up for preservation, on the verge of crystallization, whose bones decalcify, could collapse at any moment, like a pillar of salt, doesn't. Like Jacob, wrestling with his angel, rides its captor; on, on, weathering the storm, riding the singular wave, driving it home, holding the reins.

Steadfast and stalwart, clings for dear life, neck bent back, chest outstretched, teeth bared, eyes well nigh to popping from the sockets, cheeks drawn back, nostrils flaring, limbs contracting, veins near to bursting, muscles constricted, vasculating—

Seizes the oars! Draws forth his sword and plunges to the hilt: bursts forth, shedding the still-writhing skin of the shell of the other, that had encased him, this vast expanse of space and time; he had traversed! Emerged, not shirked nor shrunken by captivity, but grown, enlarged by the fight: overcome resistance in the darkest night.

He now walked forth, into the goodly light of day, and breathed new air into his soul.

AN INQUIRY INTO THE NATURE OF VICARIOUS EXPERIENCE OR, TO KILL A MOCKINGBIRD REVISITED

The subtleties revealed at close observation of the nuances contained within the nature of vicarious experiences, expose a host of manifold influences, toned-down, as it were, by would-be remnants of what-were-once colors: hues thereby deprived of that essential sense of motion which gives and takes away life, or more accurately: consciousness.

To cite an instance:

Barely opening my eyes, I lay in bed, glanced at the clock, unconsciously noting the time, caught a glimpse out the window, through the corner of my eye, grasped an impression, briefly contained it, and let go the reins, falling back to sleep.

After several such typically characterized attempts at rousing myself from reverie, I arose, lifting body from bed, head from pillow, I entered the day, not bothering to actually awake.

"I Went Through The Motions," was the name of the dance in which I was engaged to participate, peripherally.

Eyes turned open. In the front of the back. We watched with awe. The sound of the tear-box opening. The dirge of the drill. The test of conversation.

The pill-box for the summer. Thorn essential: bridge of pendulum. Denseness of the desk in-between you and you. Distortion more than occasional. Accuracy of insulation. Disturbance of doves. Formation often distant. Configuration offers testimony. "And WHOM are you?" is the name of the process of naturalization, the extent of which to-date has relieved the emotions of responsibility of its own destiny. "So you want to be a SOMEBODY," said the voice inside the collar. "Then how do you account for the fact of infiltration of the first degree?" retorted Tension Deceiver.

Notice is made of the conversation between the Tax-Collector and the Missionary-Man. One hears more than was desired. There is no going back. There ARE central themes. New haven for the "Esoteric Chic," involvement with whom cannot but make for increased comprehension of each other's natures by separate nations. Individual authors prove less innocent in groups. Inventory is the key. The solution of invention abates the precision of masons.

There is a tree in the middle of a cloud in the sky that says it is purple and floats delicately down the hole in the ice where there is a face that seems blue and which says I am a face in the ice which seems blue and I am really not what I seem to be I am really a tree in the snow or a cow on a fence in the middle of night or a white white coyote or a pussy-cat in the snow or a spoon left out in the rain or a ceiling which refuses to melt or a red clay ashtray that closes its mouth on itself through the gold-flecked leaves or tear-drops in the snow or ice-cubes in the snow or refrigerators in the snow or ash-trays in the snow or pre-destined rectangles in the cold white snow the old white snow the old gray snow the old black snow the snow in wintertime that blows its nose the snow in wintertime that blows its cool the snow in summertime that bends to the growth of the soil which knows the goody-goody- gumdrops in the snow the Howdy Doody in the snow amid the barking of candlelights in the glowing heart of the snow itself the keeping of a diary from right angle. I never thought about things like that.

I talk so loud I can never hear my thoughts: I am awake again, and I was never even asleep. I speak so softly that a brook runs through my hands; my mouth is captivated—and I can see you from where I stand.

I sit alone and speak to no one: there is someone

else here. There is no one else there. There is something somewhere.

There is a mountain near me. And a spotted cantaloupe. An ear-muffin dragon and a spear-contorted fresco. A lemon quarried answering machine, and a leather-engraved cistern tree. A fortunate butterfly's dream-book, or a box of wish-bound tributaries. Soul of some spinach. Just sign on the dotted line.

There is a tree in the middle of my eye, in the middle of the sea, in the middle of a rainbow (in the middle of my thoughts), in the middle of my throat, in between parentheses, in the middle of a thesis, in the middle of another tree, in the first place, in the last place, and the next-to-middle place. In my throat heaves a sigh: leaves turn green from brown, and then back to brown from green again; without hesitation minds turn backwards and sideways creep along the fountain of indecisiveness. Tremors tremble in the wake of unseen floods. Books open, and close (having remembered appropriately, the slim appeal of monosyllabic words).

We work toward some fine expression. We move in mysterious and various ways. No glim groves grow within the salt of wounds gone by.

Signposts awaken and signposts glisten in the moonlight. We awake to find our trees have grown to ashes, our thoughts have grown to trees, and our ashes have grown into sheep. Our hearts have turned to minds, our minds have turned to heat, our heat has turned to eyes. Our eyes have turned to thoughts, our thoughts have turned to robin's eggs. Robin's eggs have turned to robins and robins have turned to robin's eggs. Robin's eggs have turned to robins, and robins have turned to robins. Nests have turned to skyscrapers (oops), skyscrapers to eyelashes. Furniture returns to nature, fur returns to whom it belonged. Lampposts turn to fish. Gas makes goldfish. Windows press inward. Outcasts turn around. Latecomers change to chairs.

Gardens press flesh. Density creates beds. Fortune spins globes. Horses treat of parsnips. Ground hovers madrigals. Wainscoting knows dandelions. Test tube rings bells. Fog dances. Tenderness moves chains. Walls change corduroy. Tables defeat darkness. Torture inflicts debutantes. Salvation warms handiwork. Sobriety kindles harmony. Dalliance awakens doom. Dormitories press secretion.

Telepathic dogma, drives me from the house; we stand outside, drenched dry in our own-juices'-suit. Our selves are not content to be contained. The light is still on. We can hear the sound of footsteps, which is not the same as hearing footsteps and that is not the same as footsteps. Footsteps in the dark. We hear them echoing down the hall-way, down the shady lane: and back again. The monk in the vestibule. The oriole in the tree. Patience is mindful of sanity.

So the same voice occurred again. We are eager to remember. We eagerly relive each moment. Vital signs relate great fortunes. Bare, and brittle dawn begins again another day. Somber sleep evades each eye's averted glance betraying words that wisdom comprehends.

All alone, in the fit of doom, my mouth forms syllables, of clay, rock, and amber; stone is softer. And I float from limb to limb, like star-dust; like angels' feathers in the dark of winter's night. Almighty breath breathes heat into. My eyes can-not but see. To see.

Tell me, do you see me? And I see you. Question me, for all I am worth. To explain me. Understand your-self. This is the same place. Where we stand. Now.

The sky opens up, upwards. Come float with me; very

simple. The tree branches off, and grows together too, at the same time, as well. Don't notify anybody. Don't tell. This time it's a secret; but it's no secret anymore because we know it. We elaborate our lives, we simplify our minds. The merest gestures are reduced to mere forms. Even still, you are never entirely known to me. And this is the mystery. The sweet, everlasting mystery. Love is the mystery of life, and life is the mystery of love.

They came like that. A chimera that raged until all thought moved slowly into sounds. Sounds of what. Sounds of proper toolings, moved. Moved into space. And consorted with the air. The waves on the air. Like an air poem. A poem of air. Like a farmer whose sheep have gone astray—he had to send them away. Like 9 cats. They all have lives. There is seriously no certainty or uncertainty. She had an obsessiveness with form. Of form. In the form of. Lena. Laying way back to the time. The time. The time. You want to come in. There are islands. The voices always speak. A man caught in a cobweb. Yellow stone. I want to scream for him. Touch evades thought. Concentration camps. A new kind of thought process. I am itching. There is no lie. And the sands of time sift leaves as the turquoise tortoise fled the fountain, I remembered.

The waves. Slap. Slap against the short, short shore. Bulgarian hearing aid. Telescoped thoughts. I know the taste. Like King Kong. Staying power. Caresses of the fruit. Presents. O.K. That's right. You're going to teach me about it. You can't even find them. Seed valley. From all sides. Send me away. I want to remember.

Then the man caught on the head, fell out of bed. A small child sitting on the sidewalk, and it was blind. All by itself. Translate please. Everyone has to get up. It was raining. People had to live in the house. People in them. And they could not stop, you asked them. Capricorn. Holes on either side. Just like Grandpa's house. They put chairs on either side of the bed when I used to sleep over so I wouldn't fall out of bed. This is the famous place—I don't remember a thing. Trying to get a word in edgewise. Otherwise, forget it.

Skillful, he maneuvered his life. Like a cockroach. I had to stop. Going down. Stop over the side or the edge of a gift, which is what it is.

It looks like a desert out there. I've don't this before.

We exchange material. I was amazed. Our lives become a medium of exchange. More than anything else. Touchdown. In this way, anything becomes plausible. The sound encompassed. Small things. They do not move. I thought I saw a pussy-cat. I did, I did. I did see a pussy-cat. And it moved. Toward me. She is white. At night. And that is nice. Things move. And we all heave a sigh of relief at having lived another day.

Our afflictions are transcended. In the 5th house the commotion is quelled. Do not forget me.

I told all that could be told. And still nothing was said. A piece of paper is blown along on the grass. In the grass. Over the grass. Above the grass. Through the grass. Along the grass. Around the grass. Before the grass. Across the grass. After the grass. Probably the grass. The children get so much. To the grass. Inside the grass. Saved again. Before leaving.

Through the hive of glass, like she said. How many times.

Sold on it. Sold on thought. Beginning to believe in my own thought processes as possibly being a potential source of accurate information. Resisting sleep.

Believing in eyes. Belief is a huge hump on a mountain's back. We are beginning to respond to our own minds. For the only part of exchange is meaningful that is called sharing. Cows and ducks. What doesn't remove. And doesn't cover. And doesn't uncover. Like a last glass of champagne. You know I'd give it back. Sometime.

Don't mention removal. Removal of the movement. Removal of the moment. Removal of the movement of the moment. Motion Sickness.

Sold on the beginning. The beginning of beginning. There is the dance. I fell through the floor. You could not believe it. The fire engines. Where is this coming from. You and I, you and me. Anxiety.

This man said, "I couldn't forget the look on her face."

When you saw the ceiling fall in, "What did you say?"

"I said no."

I want a hamster. This is mine. A hamster died the other day, last year, last summer, last week, last movie, last Albany, last membrane, last bust, last lobby, last onanism, last butterfly, last brother, last mold, last earring, last opening, last snowmobile, last forest, last begonia, last monster, last euphemism, last birdie, last typewriter, last business, last goldfish, last sometimes, last Presque Isle, last boom-boom, last eraser, last guitar, last fortress, last tapir, last toothbrush, last foetus, last element, last starfish, last flavor, last pillow, last amour, last form, last test, last accident, last formula, last one, last sentence, last rhumba, last try, last loss, last lamb, last tress, last tool, last hippy, last desk, last turn, last opera, last apple-sauce, last beaver, last fortune, last frost, last amber, last melody, last lease, last egg, last cargo, last friction, last door, last list, last antenna, last antelope, last ant-eater, last cupboard, last tree, last lingering, last document, last end, last tunafish, last movement, last destiny, last tubular hallway, last lesion, last tentacle, last anchor, last timber, last engine, last distinction, last destruction, last dune, last motor, last kiss, last eye, last red, last letter, last loam, last dress, last litter, last mouth.

There was a man who lived with a dog. They lived in a house in a lake. Toom-toom! How can you say such a thing? You know now what this means. Beg. Beg for it.

Beg and steal for it. You can hear me? Why do you turn your face away from the gray gray day? You are free to move, free to move around. There is no door that is closed to you. You have all the potential for a great beginning right now. So hold out your hand and kneel on bended knee for a morsel, a crumb, a beverage. My jaw is sore. You can not spit your teeth out. Out of my mouth, and the squirrels are out again for food. Looking for food. We smell. We know what we are looking for. The world is run by men and men propagate their fantasies upon the whole world. The world is an extension of men's fantasies. Try and see it in any other way, and you are doing the same thing. Talk about it. Talk about it to someone. "I've seen enough," he said as he lowered the shade. Lowering the boom. Rustle up some hogs' eggs. Will you remind me not to repeat myself when possible in a girlish movement monumental gestures open drains of thought, so long clogged with the sludge of ancient mysteries.

We have forgotten. The sun beams through the clouds, through the window in the clouds. Through the window of the mind in the clouds. Already she has the perfect stewardess/waitress mentality. Are you angry? No, I am only collecting my thoughts, as some people collect butterflies in their stomach aches and pains in the liver are not the same as cheese and crack our crack are crack a check or crackers, and return the compliment.

I wanted to see what you could do, since 10:30 this morning. Let me get married and open the window. The window is a jar. The door is a jar. The apple is a jar. The smoke is a jar. The anticipation is a jar. The conch is a jar. The fish looks like a jar. The pin is a jar.

The foot used to be a jar. The fortune was a jar. The envelope has a jar. The tender varmints have a sudden, unexpected jar. The Indians have had a jar. The turn of the century could use a jar.

The liquid looks of daydreams make dents in my head. Thank you for asking. Tender loving care. Take care of yourself. Whole self. Don't be afraid. Rumble rumble. The rumbling of a train rumbling down the track; train down the track, track down that train!

"Open the Ivory Coast to visitors," the tourists say in Antarctica and Pluto. Rumble loud, louder, loudly, loudest of all. You can tell him by the ink-stains on his feet. You can tell him by the mountains in his veins, which like funnels, reminisce upon the old wooden days of long ago. They were streets, then—there were no golden dogs. Upon where the cat sits the cat. On the other side, nobody, Can say? What what do Lou-Lou-Belle do about it. Change places; "Turn the wheels off the floor, you buzzard!"

"Forget about it."

There, pins dropped and no one was the wiser. Cool lymphs moved down the farthest reaches of turn, dented plate cases upon the ruin of dimes'-tooled-chicken-ticking. Over and out.

There, upon the window ledge which we looked out of onto the only vacant space in sight (the lot across the street), we leaned; our elbows raw to the bone, our eyes glued to their lids, and Faith (liquid counsellor of bypassed dreams of unopened childhoods), humped over our shoulders, like a great wooden yoke, for carrying water. We stood, leaning on the windowsill, and endless days rolled by, following endless nights in a pattern of motion.

Following a pattern of motion, thoughts are glued to an endless pattern of movement, which the eye, like stained glass, beholds freshened in the morning dew.

Before the sun rises, flowers open.

Sea clouds full of surface, cloud surface full of seas; seas on clouds surface fully to the top. To the top of trees that hang from the roof, the roof between our knees; the knees beyond the moon that hangs in my mouth, in my room, in an unopened envelope—it shakes, stirred by the breeze, it opens, slowly, like a cloud whose sound has been disconnected from its roots, its roots between its knees, its knees that know no form beyond the folds of sheets, sheets of thought that form no mold which hangs from the roof, the roof of the door, the door of my eye that closes slowly, the slowness of clouds that pass on the horizon, soundless, like the rumor of something which has been forgotten, in less than an hour, an hour in which no residue has accumulated, in the light of a rude approach, in the form of a skeleton that has no key, like the breath of a stale piece of bread in a dish on the table that does not move, we know it is there, like a rude remembrance, we had not forgotten, we know there is no clue but the opening of a thought that clues us into a deep deep sea that destroys the quiet of a new-found slumber, we know no lies, that is what turns our head around, we don't return again.

And now it is the night again, we do not pause to look around us, forgetting the forms of things we saw before, like the tune of a breeze blowing again through the tree-tops, there is a sound in my ear, I don't know where it began but here is a view of the house, there is no window, there is no door, I told you what I said, there is no sound, there is no song in the trees, you know there is, I don't have a secret, I haven't any dinner, I don't find trees, I wear a blue star on my shoulder, in my hand there is no opening, how do you do, we don't like the look of that sky, the clouds pass overhead, I haven't any brain, the time has come for us to go, I'll go on ahead, there is a little shack in the woods, there is no opening in my eye, no matter how much it might hurt, I want to know, how could we prove it, there is no coldness in the air, and he was stopped, so he must have found out something, I don't know what it is, if he sees us, we're just taking the air, the sea is calm and undergrown, my home is in the woods, I haven't forgotten anything, there is a tree, I want her to tell us the same thing, wait a minute, there is a path through the woods, you climb up onto the rocks, there is a high mossy place, no one ever goes there, I planted a garden and hid it in the fruit cellar, I haven't forgotten, where is she, no unnecessary words, and away you go, so fast there isn't time to cry, just try to do that with a knife, everything but your fingers, like this, something must be happening, the trees are moving, I hear the sound of the sea in the distance, I know the sound, from the back of the boat we saw the rushing foam in the wake of forward movement, the ship's belly slapping against the surface of the water, the weight of wood against water, the dip and soar of gulls against the sky their features in the air, the clouds above the sea, at least in his own mind, and when reality came too close.

There is once again a surface, that moves, that runs over and runs down the steps, this does not move, the steps do not move, someone moves down the steps and into the street, out the door and into the window, over the hill and under the river, above the mountains and through the stream, far from the fountain and near the ocean, head him off at the pass. (Return to the depot.)

In the wild of the wood it screamed, having been extinct for some million years and then stepped on (we do not know why) and then there was the moon. There arrived in time of evening upon the waves, hollow wood that floats, it is grey, grey and brown and the finish worn off.

And at this, the lighthouse blinked—opened its eyes and windowpanes: ice against the martyr's dry ice. And the stars, and the stars and clouds tell stories. We had not heard before. We were not listening. They were not speaking. The speaker and listener must acknowledge each other's existence before communication may occur.

Those ice blankets, thank them. Lend in an armful doldrum. Desk arrested lent an executioner's helmet. Tends to derive distinction over air-whales. From the parked bench to over the hills we gopher turning point. For the far-begotten tartan. (Because it gives me pleasure.)

Where the wall meets the ceiling; that's where I say hello. The floor stands still. Looking like a window. There is no limit to vocabulary. Hide among the bushes.

The lustre of a wall illuminates perception. Because the light cannot come through. The door must be closed, and we are early. The chairs are sitting, face up. (To the universe.) This is where we get on. Personal hygienic habits may develop or inhibit one's writing ability. Or not lose the drift of it. "I must not explain myself." This is self-explanatory. Welcome to the (sic) room.

The first thing is penmanship. Even this reflects the male state of affairs around here. Let us say penpersonship.

THE
DECISION-MAKERS

I have made a decision. I have thereby entered into that region known as "The Realm of The Decision-Makers."

. . . and now the cold night is here: the cold night that stops and does not stop, that hears without hearing, speaks without speaking. Hear, not hear. And the globes, the globes behind the ears. The old strained night—the moon, a sliver in the black night sky. We are warm, somehow. Continuity and tranquility exist among grey laughter. We hear voices, if from afar.

In back of me sits a shadow, a shadow of the universe I left behind. A box of thoughts. Forgotten keepsakes. Lost memories. Little bits of cloth. Boxes up to the ceiling. The sound of the rain that has not yet fallen. Open the window, please. Do not let it frighten you, my child.

Go; go to the back of the room, to the back of the world, to the back of the chair where you are sitting. And without opening your eyes, tell me about the setting sun. There is no value in valor.

A man in a rainbow pulls apart aggression.

Invest bells and crevasses.

Don't remember anything.

Don't forget to use destiny.

the words you think you know do not exist.

Sneeze water.

Dis-embody form in fifteen minutes. To joke around the clocks of forcemeat. To see what he said today. Don't waste hyphens. And scrolls defend perplexity. Made in China bends for the summer's length across the field. Describe, please.

Well, in the event of the maturing of the subject, we break our backs in protest of the advent of carbon gas. Do you mean to say the open other rests for the time being closer to heaven than doubtful ingenuity?

A window floods immensity for fortune's sake and breaks the air. Don't negate possibilities. She knows all the answers. I forgot how to blow my nose. Heartbreak Hills. Rescue me from the bleeding boards on the floor.

For all time, now we learn the way to make hay turn

to dust in the flicker of an eye. Tease me for the flood of my own mistakes. Take away my absolute fear.

Touch. And the light from across the street. The thrill of an enclosed space. Waking up in the morning and knowing you are still there. Torches in the night. Lights of arches foaming under the heat of stone rocks not turned over.

When you plow up a field, there is no way to distinguish between where you have been and where you are going. This is not really true, but it seems that way when you are not plowing up a field. Annoying singing. Is like the rattling of window pain at night when it is not wanted.

There is a yell from the street. Someone fell up the stairs.

There is a wall + a window + a desk + a chair. There is wool + density. The same things in different forms. Handwritings change. There is a look of despair. There are no palm trees. There is no balance. There is a fresco in a cave. There is a farmer in a field. There is a horse in the bedroom. There is a bird in a bush. There is a four-poster electron under the eaves. There is no chance of return.

He forgot to tell anybody. No one asked. No one knew. No one existed. No one remembered. No no no no no. She saw it move. No no no. There were birds. No no no. There were cows that moo'd. No no no. No, there were no no's. No no no. Why were the birds so quiet. No one knows. Give them my regards. He forgot. No one saw me move. I told him to forget about it. In spite of everything that moves. The reflexes act. Act on account. As though no one were there. I wanted to kill them. Something forgot its own existence. It never was there. No one forgot. There was a vacuum of space. Nothing opened. Able-bodied men were moved. A horse rode into the distance. Somewhere someone took in their laundry from the line. The clothes were hanging. She was not afraid of them blowing away. Or falling down. There was no door to close. The closest thing was a clothesline. He wrote out of desperation. The night grew on. The night dropped noticeable moments from the stars, as they rowed out onto the lake.

Far from the shore, closer to the truth. Nothing forgot obsession. Do the frogs know about the winter. They must. Do the trees know about the winter. An ear infection from ear plugs. They speak softly in the other room. They think they are being considerate of me. I am sitting here writing, close to the wall, the door, and the window. The radiator is not working. I am defining a space that is defined for me by my being in it. A cough. A truck drives by outside.

Outside is not just outside, it is very far away. A window is not the only thing that separates the outside from the inside. I once lived in a little house on the west side and it seemed to me that a window was what separated the inside from the outside. It is simply not so.

What it is that separates the inside from the outside is the fact that the one who is speaking of the situation as being either inside or outside is either or neither inside or outside. One must be both inside and outside to have there be no inside or outside.

That is, if the window is closed and one is inside, one is looking out the window, which makes it be the inside and which makes the outside be the outside. If one were also on the outside looking through to the inside, one would also be on the outside, defining the situation by that division.

If the window were not there, chances are, a wall

would be there. If there were no wall there, there would be something else there. If there were nothing else there, there would be nothing else there.

I LOOK OUT THE WINDOW AND SEE ANOTHER WINDOW

Looking out the window where I am sitting at my desk, its frame painted white where streaks of brown show through and the glass is spotty and wants washing, I look out through the bent metal safety guard which has almost fallen off, with its twisted pieces curled at the top (some of which are bent outwards), and its curved pieces holding it together, I see the brick wall, which is perpendicular to this one. Some of the bricks are burnt from the fire in the building next door with varying shades of red and black patterns and the coarse, grainy cement that holds it together. Most of the bricks are laid lengthwise, but of some of them, only the ends protrude. There are a few nails and large metal hooks coming out of the wall. I don't know what the nails were for, but the hooks may have been for a clothesline. Then there is the window, the bedroom window, with the black slate windowsill. The gray window frame is old, and almost fallen apart. The glass of the window is clean and divided into four window-panes. I can see the green blanket that I put up to keep the air from coming in. One corner of the blanket is stuck outside the window, apparently having gotten caught when the window was closed.

I don't feel comfortable. This is fictional. It comes from writing on pillows instead of a desk with a view of the downtown skyline. Surely, the windows rattle and miscellaneous bumps are heard from upstairs. When someone told someone else about me, the latter's reaction was one of blankness. And we had once been good friends. This is prose. There is a blue and white angel which is a candle that looks like the sky and clouds melted together. A picture of a little girl smiling coyly at her cow. A box of white tissues and a clock that ticks. A glass which had contained boiled custard which has since been drunk. Liquid paper and India ink. I do not feel welcome, anywhere. I can not work. My mind is on the blink. This is like writing. Chocolate Pudding is a nice name for something. Chocolate pudding is what it is. And you know what happens next.

Cancer in my left brain—it's taken back I'm taken back to the other side of morning—the string-and-nightmare side of morning—the jars are broken—love floats on the surface face down on the water—the blood filters slowly down to the bottom.

The seaweeds and algae in the lake bind me together—they come around me—the water lilies and cattails bind themselves around me.

Who can say what the earth is planning to do with me—

What matters and what forges stupid idiocy in the glens. Warm kids drink milk from bags of skin that hang from the trees.

Tonight I am here in our bed alone and very much aware of being without you. My existence is not as sure a thing as I would like to think it is. I am pale and not very healthy looking.

The sounds at night out in the street press against the glass of the windows that keep us inside and what is outside out. Shadows walk around us in the distance. Amid the hurrying entertainment of the evening meal we blend our thoughts with mustard. We sit around the campfire telling old stories and jokes. The moon shines brightly. The act and sound of speech descends on us as unexpectedly as a ceiling falling to the floor; and yet, somehow as inevitable.

All the same, we cannot move from our seats. We thank them for coming so far, to see us. It was snowing so hard too. You have to walk so far from the road to get to the house. While the tea cools, we think about the day that has passed. There is not much to remember. Something about the rain. We were inspired and then let down.

We sit around the campfire trying to stay warm. Our marshmallows burn, and we forget about the wind-chill factor for the time being.

There is no noticeable change in the weather, in either direction. As in a snowstorm, then the cones and needles become covered with dust, I forget about my cares and try to relax. How interesting it is to note

The prospect is defined as the time is simply stated. The surroundings mold their variables to the source of indication within set limits. To the outward eye no disguise is accurate in place of the gesture of disillusionment. From the outside-in, it seems clear that nobody was home.

From the gate to the city, came a man who walked away from it alive. With the key in his hand, he fell out the window and down the garden path. There were no cobblestones to roll along beside him.

There were two very nice people, instead. From the mountain to the bay, we walked until morning, as the clouds lifted, and played gin rummy till noon. "Forgive the way the pedestals bend," I said with an apologetic air. "It's not their fault, you see."

From the limits of conception to the fall of inclination we received colds implying there were faulty mechanisms at work. In the calm confection of daybreak, we bowed our heads in another direction; the angle expanded by the seams on our heads.

To collect tunes like butterflies was our goal and desire. An antedated civilization was our blend of nakedness and thoughtlessness. To counteract this pattern, we thought away our problems, as the day wore holes in our feet.

When the doors close, the wall opens. When the neat's-foot oil continues, the daughters of the air waves explode. When thoughts return like beavers to the pond to rebuild broken dams, then they do what beavers do—they walk sideways like this and remove all traces from the carpet of their conclusive existences.

Can the wells of indecision overflow at the thought

of abandoned sleep? Do birds of prey rest their laurels back on the haunches of their little pangs of destiny, little stabs at happiness, little all-inclusive fudge-links to tie the ends of their voices together like the world made moveable, again?

To the cost of discrepancy, do the tape-worms of immensity move mountains of earthenware jars in Tennessee (of all the nerve)? When miraculous tendrils conclude the overtures of lust around the burnt orange navels from the sea to shining sea, across the ham-hock basin—"Look!"—there went another good-for-nothing anapest. For the meantime, look around you; when leather-jackets turn yellow, when carpet remnants press their nails in pain, when fleeing telephone booths collapse among piles of yesterday's racing forms—then you know.

Then you know the obvious answer to be true. Then the truth is cylindrical, like air waves in motion. Then the truth is rudely forgotten, like a mole, newly emerged from the snout of its own being. Then the grizzly bear converges on the little good wood in the middle of the forest hues. Then the baker, at midnight, sears through the frosting to the other side of mildew.

Casting on the shore of motion made stable, we watched the sun go where the sun goes. Then, the cows lead us mournfully home to bed. We could not see to speak; so true rang the bell, unforgotten, of yesterday's ministry. We had taken on our vocation. The blood still rushed unquietly through our veins. The hands of those who looked behind them, like alabaster, turned away from fright—they screamed down the tunnelway to the place of equidistant substance.

The books are on the shelves. The conflict is resolved, momentarily. The nuclear thermos breaks inside itself—shattering a vast array of misplaced unconnected vowels and curdled whey. The rocks took on a new substance, like poetry, attributed to various distinguishing characteristics that separated it from the run of the mill.

"There are no millers anymore." They have forgotten the use of figuring. Calligraphy is inescapable. The fingers do the writing in the end. The waves of ink—the steady flow of paper—the reams of horizontal lines— activity suppressed by rainbows. Doves that collect taxes, and do not pay their own.

A shattered piece of glass. A pearl englobed in a

sea of fiction, and by supposing anthem. The antlers of ingenuity arrive too late. The season of suspension inflates across pillars, without anyone's noticing. The fault in the ice. The growing of conclusions. The entry of ideas. The order of order.

I have been drinking fenugreek tea out of desperation—and eating fresh dill and parsley from the forest in the refrigerator—I bought five newspapers this morning hoping to find something about myself—instead I am compared to someone else—an illustrious comparison no doubt, but presented negatively nonetheless. My lips are swollen still, from the night before and I had to go out with a scarf around my face, like the Invisible Man. A man came up to me, hand outstretched for money—"Man, I don't have any money!"—"Well, don't get mad," he said—I went off muttering under my breath—"Fucking assholes."

This says to write; to sit and unwrinkle the folds of the brain till it tingles—open wounds, the light is hot—sounds from the street—I want to write till the hills come down from where they are to meet me, till the saturations of daily light extend to fill the ends of the middles of the beginnings of our minds.

Hives, not the kind they keep bees in but the kind you get on your body. Tiny red bumps; they appear as suddenly as a garbage truck downstairs that is heard through the window.

This is like a summer night—summer night in the hives of Gibraltar. The act of writing in a physical sense, is so distracting that it still takes away my attention. I want to write with the lights off so I can't see the act. I want to write with my clothes off so nothing stands in the way.

I can write as well as Hemingway or Faulkner when I want to. They carried a man away in a wheelbarrow, like a pile of rocks. The snow began to melt. That's because I've been saving it up.

Saving it up for you, babe. Piling it up for you, babe. I'm like a reservoir of love, for you, babe. Ready to give it to you, babe, when you're ready.

A house sits on the hill, and the wolves attack it—devouring everything in sight. The wolves suck bees' blood and canaries' milk for breakfast. They lunch on turpentine and caviar. Supper is sumptuous—leafy green death's heads with goldfish teeth.

I briefly look out the window in a search for vacuous

space. The approach of midnight comes steadily on. They sat in chairs, easy chairs, well stuffed and upholstered with satin. Nude to the toes, they settled into a comfortable position.

Exploring one's navel—this is the only proof of having been born. So reassuring. So unsettling. My whole life is based on being with someone, or not being with someone. A hamburger sandwich.

That is, wishing someone were there. Not being content with being alone, or with myself.

Like the stream that ran through the woods by the fireside, we woke to the sound of heavy footsteps from the hallway. There emerged a thoughtful recollection to the right of Senor's left elbow which protruded from a demure half-sleeve turned up at the end where the cuff should have been.

By the wall, sat an overcoated gentleman whose name we did not know. The boat rocked back and forth. We felt a form approaching by way of the hidden gate to the sea which often bled forth from the heart. Kidneys empty themselves profusely on the pavement, that used to be cobblestone but isn't anymore.

By Wednesday, we would have thought that

chocolate might have saved us from our other cravings. Sunny, through the refrigerator, we found a sauce of seaweed. The oven floated, turned black and fell apart, mid-air.

Do you really care if I give it away to someone else.

I was thinking of an image—and then all of a sudden it came in and lay down next to me. Space defining space. Switch gears. So long upon the length of rocks. Like lying down take the weight off your arse. Help me to understand what you're trying to say. If you have no reason to read this, don't read it. Don't take any chances. I don't. I write in longhand, not wanting to miss a word. I think of you, but decide to keep on writing anyway. You couldn't hear me when I spoke to you. You were the only person who could hear me. You understood me. You didn't understand a single word I said. I think of you, and decide to go on living anyway. I've written so many pages about you. I am writing a book about you. You are so many people, to me. I sound like Anne Frank. That's the way I feel. Notes from underground written from the sixth floor.

You are somewhere up on a swing. I write in pencil

because I am no longer afraid. You can tell what a word means by the context in which it appears. When I used to shave my head, people thought I looked strange. When my hair was very long, people thought I looked strange. A fishing rod. A divining-rod. Knowing how to use your instincts. Like a penguin on the ice. Getting your rocks off. Platypus. Eucalyptus. Koala bears. Silkworms. Mushrooms. Alfalfa grass. Pine cones. Pineapples. Star apples. Love apples. Green apple squirts. Granny Smith apples. Vermillion apples. Ostracized apples. Negotiated apples. Dietetic apples. Crystalline apples. A lesbian apple whom I wanted to fuck who wouldn't because I was a homosexual. Tut tut.

Behavior. I want to eat breakfast at two-o'clock in the morning. I don't.

Faded out blue by the beach where there was a fence by the river there was sand by the fence there was fence on the other side of the fence there was wooden fence rolled up on the beach on the other side of the fence there was sand and there was the river over the mound I couldn't see it but it was there the air was fresh and salty and cool and wet I remember it used to feel like that sitting out on the rocks by the ocean near where the waves came in you could feel them on your cheek there was a hotel or a house up on the rocks it was grey and early in the morning and I wrote a descriptive essay about it for school and I went out on the rocks on the sand on the beach near the ocean one morning very early and it was grey and cold and wet and I went and sat out on the rocks I liked to climb the rocks and I lost my watch out on the rocks and I once wrote about the watch lost out on the rocks it was cold and gray out on the rocks and I didn't know what time it was I forgot my watch out on the rocks it was hard to tell what time it was because it was so gray and you couldn't see where the sun was it was cold and wet out on the rocks and I sat there looking out to the sea watching the waves and the sky and trying to find where they met or one stopped and the other began or they both melted into each other and I lost myself that day out on the rocks and it was cold and wet and gray and I couldn't tell what time it was or who I was or what anything was

By the waning moon, by the half moon, the electrician with eyes like a cat, stalks bravely the subtle explosions that haunt the grey night at their source. Across a covered bridge, they tear apart pencils in haste, abandoning razor blades, in an effort to find something to write with. The burnt cork, abandoned in the drawer that is falling apart, signals in his mind a return to sensibility long since abandoned along with the various other remnants and last vestiges of a world we had all left behind and forgotten.

Like things placed in the drawer of a desk over which we sit, hump-backed—(not remembering what was in it)—we sharpen, through continual activity, the membranes of memory that remain, though dull, lingering like Brussels sprouts in the garden, unpicked, all winter under snow.

Objects, such as they are, to which no one could have objection; we cast a watchful eye on them. They teach us how to spell, and vastly improve our senses of what the past consisted of—the stuff of which dreams are made.

The drama of oceans, the paradox of prose—flocks of letters that move, like sheep, in herds, I shepherd them along, together. The depth of sky above us, so often spoken of—blue in all its senses—nuances of color—hues confirmed and variable—carefully formed gradations in flux continual—merry masques of woodland scenes—creatures great and small— the comforts of the wilderness—the offerings of the woods—fluttering rainbows—words that light the senses, effectively uniting the tension of young fruit trees and birdhouses. A writ of empty seashells.

We band together, like tubers that move across the ground, like ghosts or snails—I repeat I am a fish— in all likelihood. We survive somehow, through this interchange—we are not fashionable—we pull our own weight—we oppose all dogma—we rat on elocution and its cute spittoon. We cut from the bark of deciduous trees, hearty bulges, to see what they contain. We creep into the forest at night, when it is dark, to check for lost craters and claviers. We speak quietly, never raising an eyebrow. We give up our seats to quiet cats, with glowing eyes, because the village common is no longer honored. We aim to restore the rightful place to which each thing is entitled, and hope to overthrow the table of contrition and everything on it. We stoop to conquer and spare no pains in doing so. We have no hat to hang our heads on, and keep a dictionary close at hand at all times. We often begin a word with its second letter, and undisturbed return to fill in the one which should begin it. We do away with coffee and substitute chickweed, instead of chicory.

The limbs of a tree we perceive the question of dusk with open eyes. Don't forget, don't forget. Words are written. In a moment words are written. Life is a final act. Action is an end result. The depiction of life is like discolored paper, old with age. Like the face upon a window, written in glass, looks back at you. There is something outside. It stares back. Eyes reflect themselves. Looking at one another. Looking at you, I see myself. Life is so simple. A tree grows out of your eyes. It grows roots into your head. Leaves grow out of it. Like a hard pencil, wood turns into branches, from trunks that were thicker than they are. We change the angle of our penmanship. We assume a different posture. It is like relating Ibsen to Strindberg. The connection is there, but to overemphasize it would be to desecrate it in a way.

The flowers that bloom in the spring. One must find a way to describe something in a way other than by comparing it to something else. I have pains in my arms. A farm in the country. A cabin in the woods. The house rattles as the train goes by. I can hear the sound of a boat blowing its whistle on the river, at night. The distant whistle of a train at night. The sudden rush of a train going through town at night, verifying the accuracy of one's perception of it, in the distance. Driving off the road in the middle of the night into a snow bank and into a telephone cable connection box that had been buried inside it. Falling asleep at the wheel and awakening suddenly, flying off the road. Walking down the road to a farmhouse and awakening a nice old lady. Calling an emergency tower to take me home. Being dragged out of the ditch. Getting stuck in the mud. Getting a flat tire. Running out of gas. Skidding on the ice.

The sound of the rain outside the window; this is an abstraction. It is about learning how to use the symbols of punctuation and employ the elements of syntax successfully through writing. The windows are made of glass; they let the light in. We clean them to increase their property of translucence. We are uprooted by the events that occur around us. We begin each day with a renewed fervor and expectation. We speak with great enthusiasm of a new clarity we hope to achieve. After all, writing is a process of clarification. Clarification of a substance, however unidentifiable it may be, it still shows through the mist that remains where thought used to be. We try to write like someone else, like one another; like what we think writing is supposed to be like, and we don't succeed. It's like learning to be able to achieve the same spontaneity we were able to respond with when we were six years old. This is hard to retrieve. The mind does not function that way, any more.

Surreptitiously, like a goat prodding upon the weight of its legs on its legs, it leaps; tethered against the will of the sky against the fence and the possibility of rain in the face of death upon the roof which rests against the fair play of incest which we know we all can trust to the depth of solidity across the valleys from which we claim flowers born in May to delight those meadows whose shields unfold in the sun, the light of which shines exuberantly within the vestibule where we congregate in anticipation of some arrival or other event however unlikely to occur it may be; we do not lose our chain of thought; we press bright links of salvation together to make one thing; it is this that we know for what it is; it is no idle circumstance; it is no question of "to have, or not to have"; it is like a bright sudden thought suspended in yellow; illumination punctuated by thrill outdistanced through thought; unyielding past the extremities by which men claim to call themselves men; we can not lose our lineage; it is our blood; we switch on over to the other side; there is no where to let go in; the discrepancy of rainbows expresses facile tissue, well-suited for such subtle occupations as these, with which we find ourselves presently engaged; there is no pre-feed seepage; no perfect strongman; no idle, lazy scheming loafers; seafaring men were we, whose afterthought may have been buried beneath the steamer. The possibility

He escapes; foot-swollen and coughing, he moves along the beach. Having reached the coastline, that is his limit—he looks around; dark bushy eyebrows and a sudden expression of unexpected arrival. Where to, what next? crows the dawn that replenishes sighs. We have reach our limitation. Only the ocean lies before us. The truth of temptation is pardonable. The rights of tarnished knives to eat with a spoon dissuade us from further acceptance of the quality of the air. When the bus unloads and a face peers over the side, we turn our thoughts to attempts to find ways of making amends to all concerned.

The pain from the center, the non-abbreviated pain from the center of the body that does not move, from the center that does not move, this is indicative of care, and intention of expectancy, like he tears apart to share with you, and you don't try to bring it on, it would represent an attempt equivalent to suicide, like the rain that falls upon the roof, and someone knows how to write about it, I was thinking about him, there was a wall between us, I might have bridged it at first, now it may be too late, we did not think about such things, she passed by the window, maybe lying on the floor is not helping, maybe relish on a hamburger is not such a bad idea, after all, I know this sounds like a line and it probably is, but the wood grows and the tree grows, instead of thunder there were drumrolls, and in the pain of the illusion of what was there, that unit was made complete, there are no comments necessary, no invasions of privacy before midnight.

They tell you "It will stay that way"; you sigh in

disbelief. They say that "It will stay like that." You remember what it used to be like. Your lip, swollen, puffed-up like when you used to act like apes as children, realizing not that you mocked an image of your future selves: putting the tongue, as you used to do, inside of your upper lip, underneath; between the gums of the upper jaw and the lip, itself—enlarging it, suddenly—apelike, simian.

Your skin, swollen with hives, puffed-up, red and scaly—They say that "It will stay that way"—There is nothing you can do about it. You should not have tried to change the way things were. It was a mistake. You know now that things would have been well enough, left alone. There is no way back.

Life was once carefully thought out. Once it was spontaneous. Now, there is nothing, only the cold realization of existence, closing in around you. What is there to do? You don't know. There's no one you can ask. You are changed into what you never wanted to be; a monkey, left to eat the stray banana peels that have been thrown away.

You sit and look into the mirror, hoping to find some flaw in the surface: there is none. It is too late.

Perfection is not an accident. You turn your head away from the glass, and stare at the wall.

Your life passes briefly and quickly before your eyes; words you have made frequent use of, like old friends, pass across the room. You wonder how it got this way. You know there are no accidents; no mistakes. Forms of bodies wander round the room, looking for something, or someone that is not there.

The endless cloverleaf of life, from which there is no exit, leaves us trapped inside the wall that is ourselves. Laughter is heard from the next room. But there is no way to get to the next room. There is no door, so the room is not next door.

Somewhere there is a hotel lobby with yellow wallpaper. Colors effect things in subtle ways. Life is in essence, invisible, and you are invisible also. There is no way to be invisible to others, though.

Life is demagnetized existence. Being is bent on destruction of itself. It is as though fulfillment can only come through a death of some kind.

I am not necessary to her. I am necessary to myself. In a particular sense. We live in little holes of air that are holes in air where there is no air. To breathe, we turn inward. To see what is there, to see what there is to breathe. We press heavily upon ourselves, and then more lightly as we go along. We don't go anywhere, really. We could not if we tried. We are in wheelchairs, when we are most mobile. We have mechanical limbs that we move through internal muscles that we push and pull like buttons in an elevator. We breathe heavily, or not at all. We don't overdramatize, but in our effort to subdue, we tend to miss the object we are aiming for. We leave the world behind and claim innocence of all its errors. We are depraved and notorious; we left whatever scruples we had left, behind us. We have no money—we would not know what to do with it if we had some.

Life has a theme. When the savants (those who know) thread their needles, there is no pain. When morning becomes electrified and there is no needle, she is the needle's eye. She is somewhere over near the river, the water flows by her door. She is the doorway to the river. I have seen her. When there is little light, she still shines brightly. When others are cold, she is still warm.

The envy we feel in the presence of the snow. A dog

that is tied up in front of a house down the street barks as you walk by no one know you and you're on the other side of the railroad tracks, we don't live there anymore, oh yeah, we don't live there anymore, none of us live there anymore. The blue elephant. You trudge through the snow for bread and butter. The simple things in life are the ones that are hardest to get or forget. Little islands that are far away from home where I am all alone. Right now.

Now something has been made clear. There are reservations where there would be floods. Thorough masquerades are reduced to thick depictions of a deeper sort, and the help of tenderness is enlisted where it is needed most.

Like the thought of night, advancing slowly toward the daybreak that approaches us: we are not home. We slip politely out the quiet door through which we came. We had not exited, as we had not entered.

The inconsistencies, which had beforehand seemed so slight, now showed another side of themselves. We whip around the darkness in despair. We talk to ourselves without addresses. We undertake great emphases.

Like the falling sound the snow makes, falling, like the sound snow makes, the sound like snow makes falling, sounds like snow makes, falling, like the snow falls, sounds are made like falling sounds, like the snow makes, the snow, like falling sounds makes fall, like sounds that make the snow sound, the snow that falls like the snow.

Considered in this light, that is the light of the moon that shines beyond the gate, beyond the glass, beyond the window, everything that has come before exists as a preparation for that which is to come, to follow, to occur; the moon has islands and oceans; there are shapes that dance around, on the surface of the moon, on the face of the moon; everything seems to exist as a preparation for what has come about; everything appears so inevitable; amazement is quelled through a quiet acceptance of the continuity by which life forms itself, through which we take form, together; the stream of life that flows throughout our souls forms a common point of interaction; things come together; the moon and the earth exist; they move together, and individually; life moves, and the people move within it, it within them, within one another; people sing and dance together; they dance around the moon; they swim inside their bodies, and each other's; they illumine one another's lives; they give love; they receive love; they feel the motion of the tides within their bodies; movement comes from the moon; there is an intuitive knowledge within us, there is a knowledge of someone who you are about to get to know; once you know them, you know that you have always known them; they know that they have always known you'; it is as though everything had been a preparation for this; the moon inhabits our minds, and our bodies; there is a part of us that has been the moon, that is the moon; a molecular warmth that moves in the blood, silent and steady; like horses that move in the rain, a little; our lives are like a field, and we are like horses that stand in it, and move, a little, when it rains; sometimes we know what to expect, sometimes not; it is a feeling of having lived a life together in another time, another world, where the world was calm; the house was quiet and the world was calm; the moon shone in the sky, and was visible through the gate on the window; and then when one looked up again it was not there; at least you could not see it anymore; someone was there, in the world outside the window, and it felt as though one had known her before; in another life, in another world; this is a secret world, the one we live in; we live in it together; it is the world between two people; it is the way they know each other, the way they learn about each other, and remember things they knew before, that they had forgotten; there is a space in which two people exist; they can go there when they want to; the space is there, and they can be there anytime; the doors are open and the windows are clean; there are smiles on their faces, they are happy; when they smile together they are sunflowers opening to the sun; they feel the moon; deep within their bodies; there is something that glows, something that is warm, and comforting, that gives balance and continuity; something that gives life and happiness; they go on, the moon goes on; the flowers go on; the horses in the field and the rain go on; the summer goes on; the night goes on; we don't forget what we have learned; we feel good and then we smile; we are happy and content; the sound of the earth moving is something we feel in our bones; we melt into the earth, like rain; we evaporate, gently, and rise into the sky together; we turn into a cloud that turns into the moon; we smile, and make the world happy, again; we curl up around one another like a cat curls up around itself; we are weightless, and we rise up, counting sheep along the way; we float above the ocean and feel the cool spray from the waves below us; we turn into apple and cherry blossoms; we become a wild strawberry plant, sending out vines all over the field. We become rocks and mountains; we become ponds and streams; we become a wild iris in the cool camp earth, in the shady places and the marshy ones; we become a dog-tooth violet and a live-for-ever in the woods; we become a fiddlehead fern and a marsh-marigold; we become mushroom and lichen; moss and evergreen.

Turns blend fall into through open eyes tender fancy leaps across to feel her open gesture as equalizing movement facet breathes along the length of lillilisbatracting forms thatabaractor whatyacoomarillowopendectomila placebegetabilitilsmacromatopsilatiapelmacrancicabinetechnicalistic

Less and less and concentration and individually & meritoriously (find the word) & deliberately & bi-annually & not festooned with & descriptively & paleolithically & like a rainbow in disguise & wear and tear & which way home & descriptive rainbows & bags full of beans & greenness in the twinkling of an eye & alienation & onomatopoetic disturbance & don't stop to linger & fixing things & mysterious clambakes & investigative enterprises & destructive young youths & toothless disintegration & memorable non-entities & variable speed life-savers & hungry ghosts & hungry ghosts & hungry ghosts & flotillas in the aftermath & elucidating rainbows & destructive enterprises & perpendicular advantages & admirable interests & conflicting viewpoints & don't kick my ass & don't kick my ass & and don't you know what follows & then & fortunately & tense & peeling & darkness & fortune & variance & density & discretion & nobility & vacuous & toe together the outward angled vantage points to fool the catfish Wagnerites with a hey-nonny, nonny no hey-nonny, nonny and I thought how brave everyone will think I am, then I'll tell them all to go to hell and then where will we be? Pushing strings and pulling buttons. Dee dee dee dee dee.

We create a space or a sense of one where endlessness takes the place of commitment. In the storage-house of anachronisms, we wash down window-washers by the dozens. They fetch good food down the throat. We write each word as if our lives depended on it, and they do. We savor every bite—crumbling tadpoles on like salt in the wound.

Avocados take root, and finally send forth shoots—this is a description of a place without a name. I watch myself silently, from the ceiling above me, as I sit writing these words. Perched as in a crow's nest, we work diligently together in our separate lies.

That is no mistake. Coffee is a word. You take your laundry to build it up and it gets washed down again. He went to the beach and left the window open. Someone climbed over the fence and went into the house. There was no one there. He couldn't find what he was looking for. He left the house, disgruntled.

It's like writing a new word that you never have written before for the first time. There is no dishonor in life. Other than the dishonor of dishonor. One destroys honor which must then be built up again.

We used to go and look in the store that sold all kinds of pink and white wicker things on the Upper East Side, together.

Don't forget to wave hello. Hello. The eyes attempt to freeze; they melt, instead. I wonder.

This is what had happened. It had rained and someone had not walked across the street. The light was changing, severely. He waited at the curb where he stood, standing at the curb where he stood, waiting; waiting for the light to change, so he could go across the street.

Suddenly, the street opened up; time opened up, and the space around him parted like the Red Sea. The earth stood still. Suddenly, everything was silent—it was like a movie projector that stopped on a single frame. Nobody moved.

It seemed an eternity, and yet there was no way to tell the passage of time, until it started again. Like a merry-go-round, it wound itself up and began to move once more.

It was as though nothing had happened, and yet he was aware that time had elapsed, or rather, that he had entered into and emerged from some kind of pocket in time, some slight discrepancy which existed in the fabric, some discontinuity that waited in the wings of circumstance, to trap those unsuspecting victims who themselves wait for such holes to fall into.

He was one such individual. It was as though his entire life had been geared toward that moment. He submitted nobly.

What is left; we turn away from the truth that looks us right in the eye through which we stare blindly like a hole in the ring-dove's neck that has been shot and pierced through it. The meek shall inherit that shake through the quaking mistakes that for episodes we rebel against. We understand but we forget. We get dizzy and slip away. We lie down and sleep it off. We would masturbate in the shower but we don't have a shower. The terrible fuss about day dreams; nobody bought a newspaper. What's all the fuss about? Broccoli in the refrigerator (i.e.: he bought a refrigerator). We were waiting for the phone to ring, or for someone to knock on the door.

Yankee Stadium fills someone's fantasies for the day. The death of death. Ball games that shoot through the eyes at you. They swing wooden bats and my blood pumps quivering through my veins. I am not going to die.

Where the glasses went then fell across the to see if they could stay along the line.

In the thick of it yet dwelled in which to dismember the memory limb from limb to statued potter reach far from the standard silk to geld the thinner strands that remain, glaring out the glass of the original motel bill we walked with whipped cream all over oh thank you and once in a great while when the whistle blows out though he had an audition so he really must have an audition.

When the cantaloupes are ripe they will sit on the shelf. And the candles will blow the cold wind out on its nose. In canvas, the colors are odors. The stationery store that rents mules. The pictures in a dictionary. Throwing up. Sitting in an arbor in a vineyard. A haven from the world's tumult. Risen from the grave. Violets that speak. The color gray. Two different spellings. Overlapped decisions. You are different.

Looking over my shoulder. You have the same pen. We could talk about that. But it was someone else. Instead of talking, why not write? Learn something from the process of salting. For preservation of food.

Pickling spices. I'm certainly not going to stay on this level. Carried me across; the Nazis—that's it. The cherry grove comme ca. Right through from Krakow. I'm starting to write like him.

Hands that move above you—steadily, stealthily, steadfastly—you are up in arms—movement occurs as a response against repose—it is the opposite of the opposite—things bite you, they make you itch—you scratch them back—what is skin—it is what we have because we don't have fur—or little pink ears—we get too cute—Kitren—she is a fish—with a little pink nose—she jumps up on a chair—she is not the blue dog—she rests her head—and if you sit in one place long enough your feet grow into the floor—it sounds like a good idea—so go do it—eat in a Japanese restaurant that does not use monosodium glutamate or sugar, and then come back later—we go and sit in front of it—we cover our breath with our hand—the smile across your lips—finish reading the things you did not finish reading this year—it is almost officially the summer—when we oil our hair and shorten our suspenders—they shorten the sentence

You keep on writing because it is what you do. You don't know what will come of it, and suddenly she is gone—she did it for us all—do the people understand what it means, understand the implications—to go out dancing, and not say what you mean—no one would ever think to look at my writing to know what I was feeling at a particular time. Well; just better give them leave to go. It couldn't be helped.

They come in floods: in flocks. They leave their mark on everything they touch and this guy is studying ballet. She is so tender. Between the shoulders. A gas mask, an oxygen tank. He fills her up and checks the oil. Someone moves around garbage pails. In the middle of the night. Moody's mood for love.

Let me reach you. I know this sounds inane but let me anyway. He only came along for the ride. The roller derby. Derby Line. We crossed the border into no-man's-land. We got the car stuck in the sand. On a peninsula. There was a ferry. There were coast guard men with suspicious boots and a lighthouse taken for granted: it was built to be blown up.

Teenage romance. Thriller. I bought him a beer. The syncopated thrust of the pelvis. A mark that shows through. Like a lamb. She stood on her two feet.

Swaying back and forth and he will kill me. If I don't watch out.

They are like swans. It gives me goose-flesh to think of it. A house by the river. Blow it up. You make me want to dance with you. My most secret places. Ashes. I can hear them. She told me.

I was left out in the cold. With my poems in one hand and my penis in the other. An egg-cream. Thank you.

Someone remembered me and someone else didn't. Why wouldn't he come out. He wanted to go away. Slowing down the process. You wanna come with me, we'll slow down the process together. The harp-weaver. Clarinets. The big one.

I am a parcel. You float away. Tenses and persons change like laundry lists. Up-tempo. Broaden the horizon. The wealth of possibilities. The warmth of the body.

We let the plains meet the sea, the way starfish meet the ocean, and antelope eat the stars. We let bygones go away in peace: we remain to drink water from white bowls on the floor. Milk comes from these. The porous substances that give out a faint odor of fungus. Wood turned to moss. Lichens that stand still in the rain. We grow around ourselves, around each other.

Like plants; they hang from brackets on the window-frame. They look out the window. They keep us posted. We sing them songs. They hum along. The animals are their friends.

We wake up in the morning, and go to bed at night. We wake up in the morning, and go to bed at night. Morning glories open in the morning, and close up at night.

In circles, we move across the room. There are wrinkles in the floor from the soles of our feet. Be careful. Magic. Surprise. A fleet of boats. Leave the massage. It hurts. Like a snakebite. Tell me how it is chestnuts. In July. Sing me a lullaby.

The thing that flattens out and whisks away the space around it; lessens the movement in the long run necessary to complete a gesture, and there she is: the one with the little pink toes is here.

The small grass grows in the little green place. Learning to write is like learning penmanship all over again, learning to see again. I called you on the telephone—you could not hear my voice—I was not speaking.

A finger pointing to the moon. The face behind the face behind the face. Someone is crying. And I cannot help her.

A small voice wanders. I look back, not in anger, but with a sigh. The clocks are all wrong. My glasses are slipping off my nose.

She leans her head against my leg. I put my head on his lap. They spoke on the telephone. We wore nightgowns. I brought dried flowers from along the highway and she liked them.

We went out and stood in the rain, he and I, in the garden, and got wet. We went out and ran in the rain, she and I, in the street, and got wet.

None of us knew each other. Some of us now know each other, but it is too late. Too late for making mobiles. Mobile sculptures. We cut things out of paper. Nituke vegetables. Dandelions. Twigs. Three-year-tea.

Thanks. Brain-food. Sex-food. Food for thought. Passe compose. Learning how to spell. The small rains down shall rain.

The sudden "Mr." event. The unexpected tubercular inclinations. Someone in a dream reveals possibilities at hand in the waking world. Fish.

Stretching the truth.

When the walls start to close in and by mistake they start to breathe instead by any stretch of the imagination my words lag behind my thoughts a little I was out on the highway in Canada I was walking along the road I went down into a ditch I was floating through the cold grey skies like a clam like a soft-shelled cloud instead of humming the wind whistled through the space between my bones my lips swelled up my hair bristling on and my skin broken fingernails bleeding and they say I am impossible they don't know the meaning of the words they use things are alive and the sound which moves like whales like centipedes across the stars sends chills the closed doors of my body the tremors of morning sent down into the fishes of our love we exist on plankton we fetch a tidy sum to curb the coast of calories we set fires on purpose and burn the ultimate versions of horns honking in the night the water overflows and she steps into it it subsides the walls grow outward we shut our eyes like books they are astonishing aren't they round and beaded at the nipples bulging fantail grosbeaks speak to us I stay alone I am also alone a cup of soup now and then he gave me money for it where does it end there is a disguise that is hanging in the closet you cannot wear it you cannot be produced and go off to Venezuela.

The fortress subsides; growth is inhibited by weeds in the dust—brush away your fears, and move on into the thrashing waves that spin around the rocky cove like sparking openings in a dense undergrowth of foreign languages which we may have heard throughout the years, with or without intending to.

Don't ever write sentences like this again; the decision is firm. It is the devouring of a quartered broiled chicken in the park at dusk with milk. We remain seated. Bones stick out. The comedian as a backwards 6. Try that on for size.

People put their arms in things and make buttons. Make with the buttons. Don't scare me off. She doesn't scare easily.

Then there is nothing to say except goodbye. And then the fish swim around the room, and then the ones with stars in their mouths close up, probably. The length of things is longer than the length of things which is longer than the length of things that are longer. The longer lasting pen is the longer lasting pen is the longer lasting pen.

The stomping feet that shake the floor and then I would feel trapped as I do now so what's the difference anyway. I can't say it. It doesn't matter anyway because I'd rather switch than fight and here she is again licking her little pink tongue and I hadn't even realized how much in fact I'd been affected by it all.

In the face of the possibilities which we face, we shrink from the thought that glides across our faces— the possible thrust of fire and egg that makes us tremble in our shoes—we enter the place of worship from the rear—there is no end to this life—the empty shelves upon the wall—the life that waits and does not begin until after we leave to open itself to us like a breakfast in a hotel restaurant before departing onto the highway at sunrise to hitchhike southwest toward one's dream.

Just because like fields of flowers, we perspire for a reason—we can see—the thought remains—we inflict guilt upon ourselves and one another. We remain to be seen—we live another day to eat another lunch—we cut each other's throats—we step across the boundaries of existence—we do not stop to kill ourselves—we open every door before we close it—we step across the threshold of immortality—we make vast gains toward immortality—while life, white and finite, creeps up beside us, and unexpectedly leaps into the void—leaving us where we are.

Like helicopters, something savage in us moves away—we are left in a uniform state—wanting what we don't have, not wanting what we have.

When fields collide like luminous pendants we partake of the sliding lights that take part in the cold limp sky that which hangs like a whale or a corrugated cheekbone in the sand-dust of the sand-dunes which no one understands except you and I and they are miracles and we can perform them in the sky in the palms of our hands at the world's end we greet ourselves as we would another that great clam-bake in the sand we understand now no fish-hooks thread our fingers when I ask you to respond you open your eyes to me and I look into the floating seas which appear between your parting lips it is the sun the moon the ravished face of earth to-be yet born inside your blossoming thighs I fly.

No one knows the pause between thoughts that mingle and intermingle like a string across the sky that harbors thoughts in guise of memories we pull apart the curtains that separate us one from the other the way fog separates sheep I run barefoot into your arms and it is raining and I am learning to see clearly for the first time in my life you are so near.

The spiritual afterglow of thought which moves like the moon within our minds we turn corners of pages in pavement round the bend we wait for nobody when the bell rings we open our eyes and come out glowing.

I feel the thought of you in the small of my back something moves, in the recesses of the imagination the skin gurgles and this is interaction transcending space there are no barriers I want to kick off my shoes I said that I had wanted to since I had walked in you said why didn't you.

No need for excuses loosen the reins the door is open pass through.

In the ancient ancient rivers send the mollusks over the counter a birth from the first seal loose upon the waters of mirth beyond which catfish stream through passages that were found to be attributed to as far as the act is concerned is a fact as connection can permit I walk across the Sunday stoop awaken the force that bends dim glasses 'gainst the ending unending motor of essence repeated internal phantasm worth dispersing across the endless gubernatorial everyone stays in each other's cabinets ask them on ice in enrage floats up endless wear bargain foot as loop in fresh of poor task into deep sleep will affirm against storms mere been pyramid weight of accentuated linen 'mid thorn and blackberry who tills dense autonomous lenders instead of white-toast we bring barter to tend the white sheep of our listening dry wheels that pass through the mountains and fences that close from an unending use which bends cows and unearthing to hardware like jello that warbles in the night we pick berries in the dark like canoes we eat carrots do you like your mattress do you spread butter does affection displease you hadn't you better lose something in a handshake and impressions of the sundriest accessories this is an order and immense legal injustice I want to reject it.

Suddenly the past is opened up before us—the sidewalk is gleaming in the near-to-midnight air of things around them—I used to work for a dancer—I don't anymore—I used to go for walks in the rain with an umbrella—there was a mystery to things, a sweet intriguing mystery—the paint is peeling off, it's starting to flake—I once walked down a road with a dog—I walked down many roads with many dogs.

I can't go on. I am sitting here going on and I can't go on. Squeezing the last drop out of myself. The sun burns my flesh—I am cooked like a piece of meat. Luckily, for me, the rain comes just in time.

There was no time to get to the ocean, not time enough. Soon there will be time enough to get to many oceans. We climbed over a fence into the woods—We walked along a brook. We drank from the water. We bathed in it.

I used to work in a bookstore—I used to drive a man around in a car and bang into things. I once drove a truck. I drove a taxicab. I have driven a tractor. I have never driven a motorcycle, although I have ridden on one. I never have piloted an airplane or motor or sail boat, although I have gone on them. I have ridden bicycles and roller-skates and skateboards. I have Ice-skated, though not very well.

I can talk on the telephone, although not usually.

Let this be a symbol of newness—like the slightly curving arch or the slightly arching curve of a leg in the wind or the hair of a beautiful woman. This waits until it is uneasiness like the vanishing arches of figs on trees that hang there, waiting to be picked. Like the curvature of a spine that disappears or is accentuated, according to the appropriateness of the occasion. Like love, that swallows willows; gives out of itself, and connects by way of continuity, the metaphor of existence. The vast fraternity that sits upon the rocky road of time sends us together through air and water—solid matter drifts away; that is, the waterways open.

I was in the round across the hills where the feet meet the mountains and swans turn to silver. They broke up pieces of wood into contrivance. In a church there was a building like a castle. Hives were not the kind where bees are kept.

Learning to perfect my vehicle. I step on heads in the meantime. And a woman walks by who looks like a man, and a man walks by who looks like a woman. In the quiet open spaces where the fields continue endlessly together

A chance to lead a disembodied existence once again. For a little while, at least. This is such a luxury. Like when the cat had to have its hair shaved away to be spayed. The skin shows through. Life floats away. It doesn't go anywhere. Seaweed, suspended in pond or water-lilies, like the ones the dog pulled up—they have those funny things that keep them afloat, but also keep them anchored.

I don't know how to do those things with people. I am the alienated martyr of my race. I cry the way other people laugh, or at least I'd like to. I give away pens—I have nothing to write with them. I cut the wood of pencils down with razor blades. I sandpaper them to make them sharp. I draw dense and ugly pictures in muddled colors. I would like to let the windows get so dirty I couldn't see out of them.

I collect rocks; big ones, small ones—I like to hold them in my hand. They ae cold at first. Then they absorb the heat of your hands. They draw out tension. Someday people will realize the healing value of this.

When I think of the hundreds of thousands of pieces of paper I have filled up with words, I am encouraged. I regard their firm blue lines, unyielding red margins, and brilliant white backgrounds with admiration. This paper is made of cells of trees turned into pulp, just like my words are written on them.

I am not afraid. I am once again alone in a room in a house where I live. It is quiet. The cat is in the other room. This is a different house than before; a different cat—things change, but not really—they only substitute. One cat dies, another takes its place. You leave one apartment, and move into another. Windows take the place of windows; doors of doors; walls, floors, and ceilings of their like.

And there is the moon—the orange moon outside the window—my old friend—it is always there. I am always here. The moon and me—we keep showing different sides of ourselves—or is it that people always view us from a static vantage point—we're really there all the time. We don't come out and then go in again.

So many rooms, moons, windows. A white cat on a white blanket. I feel like a turtle in a bowl like the one I had when I was a child. I can smell the distinctive turtle smell that is so hard to characterize. Mildly sweet; humid-earthy, like a fungus in the woods.

I am a turtle, I think. I move slowly, on all fours. I eat little algae and little green things. I am a turtle.

I say this over and over again to myself. No one else believes it. I am also a raccoon and a bear and lots of other things. I do not pick these at random.

I turn things around to see a different side of them. I look to see if something's nibbling on me, thinking I'm a plant by mistake. I am very small—and I am really a turtle.

The sudden shape of midnight rounds the forms of roads that walk across silence, and compose rare trains of thought upon the dusty brow of midnight. Midnight who transfers walks of life into musical whimsies and all kings crow at the dark in spiteful eloquence. I cannot find the razor blade, although I know where it is. The sandpaper is beyond my arms' reach, although I confess my indecisiveness about it. Like eating eggs benedict beneath a black umbrella in the morning, as though this gave you an excuse and made up for meaning in the eyes of conflict of birch trees. Words we dare not mention clothed. We ask for indulgence for them. We write in pencil once again. We share opulence with sardines and open mouths with food to feed them. Seashells sit upon the shelf in a jar she got to keep them in. No one stops there. One sits upon a stand. One yells out in the street. One waits for a sign from pumpkins. One is amusing. One is amused. One is impressed with the chance to speak to one again. One collects sand-dollars and then goes looking for them. One goes blind from having sand thrown in his face. One walks by somewhere where one had been before. One remembers full moons over lakes. One plunges headfirst into the abyss. One uses salt.

Let's put the sharp knives facing down in life so no one cuts themselves, so that any blood that may be spared from flowing, may. The fact that blood is blue makes gateways creep within their paths to cherry orchards and lend their lemons to gas the onions. No one crawls where no one leans on the railing, not called parapet to avoid pretention.

Where someone calls a name out loud at night and hisses whisper fenugreek sighs in intricate alabaster, then I shift my load to the other shoulder and interest myself in the craftsmanship of art. How many people work among the roses causes blood to flow through my veins now, undisturbed.

I remember thoughtlessness turned to gravy on a

hot meat sandwich. A man who carried meatballs down into the basement. A woman who yelled after someone that he'd better not break any thing in her basement. Missing buses. The great loss. Your honor. Got it.

This is the telling that disengages thought from fiction and changes the color of leaves in autumn before the rain has gotten to them. This is what molds our thoughts to memory; quells bubbles in the stomach; turns thoughts to embers. This prevents us from searching desperately on all fours for something outside of ourselves beyond the shadow of motion that encourages us to change position, and gives a new slant to things.

They say goodbye to see how many holes they can punch in how many pieces of paper at once.

The constant shift and gurgle—he turns off the television set to go to bed. He crawls out of the hole.

Because of the floundering movement we attribute to the bait that is cast before the hook: Did you speak to her?—Who, I? . . . Speak to whom?

The enviable attributes (i.e.: celibacy, vegetarianism, passiveness, sensitivity) all increase your chances of getting shot down in the end. One must be hard and firm; inflexible to a T.

Thus, the enviable position which we claim to desire (like someone calling "Carol!" outside the building at night; this personalizes the situation for the reader, or the listener, who, being nothing himself, beholds the nothing that is there, and the nothing that isn't) causes one to eat instead.

Kissing made her lips hurt, like a day to change the linen; we work hard. We cut out the right kidney, but that doesn't answer our question.

I am not a physical medium. Wrapped in spider webs, I remember and re-enter the orgone box. The answer presses itself against my lips.

I read the way the breath moves in and out. For a while I admired myself in the mirror and then shut out the light.

The flowers upon the bureau should have been thrown out had I not asked that they be kept a while longer. I cannot bear to see anything go away.

I remember the first time I saw her. I believe we even kissed goodbye then. Her eyes twinkle, they always will.

Goldfish in a bowl, removed from a bowl. A way of changing linen. A way of sorting out what there is to be said. A way to determine when something has been written.

They are only friends. Mushrooms are only mushrooms. Join the party, they invited. The little boys' room. I have to go there.

The way words so easily take on a life of their own, even before they are written; when they are still a twinkle in someone's eye.

The way the wind blows through a window, THE window. A perfect example of movement. It is going from one day to the next. I must write my memoirs. Some day the world will float inside my head. I know this is destined.

I wait for autumn leaves. I hope for them.

Because the rest of this stands in the way of discretion. Vanity moves along the surest path of observance. From optimum vantage points we seek and press our partner's urgent thumbprint to the glass.

We edge upon the masks of certainty. The "poet" in us moves to the other side. We jump in a lake. We like the way we look. Her name is Persephone, in Latin, because she looks like a lollipop.

I can't imagine tomorrow. There should be (and there were) swans on the lake (she is also a swan). I turn in my turnoquet. The rotisserie of longitude.

The nipples that, like shelled peas, squeeze to the touch and are crisp, exude a drop of juice like the way we felt when we found out we couldn't fuck someone we wanted to fuck. I speak of the royal "we."

We keep a little duck in the sink. This is to go with the snake in the grass when there are two "the's" in a row as in the poem "The Man On The Dump" by Stevens.

We keep in mind the things that perplex us, and then, in a fury of interest, we congratulate one another for the unexpected success of "Seward's Folly."

Because of the memory that lives near someone we know who lives near someone we know in the Berkshires. We love to include ourselves and to be included. To give wisdom on the spur of the moment, the magellanic clouds.

We love snowballs. We like the cream-filled filling of high art. We emulate and embody the characteristics of high art into our daily lives. We tell great secrets and small on the Staten Island Ferry where two lovers sit entwined in heavy sweaters, gazing out of the window and we wish we were them.

We remember queer friends of our father's who had extremely pink skin, in spite of their ages, and who wore raspberry shorts and pink shirts. We have a ruffled pillow case. We sleep on the floor, just in case.

We listen to the sirens all night and feel the breeze coming in from the window. We are interested in many things including a novel of sublimation in which the sirens continually fade into the distance.

We might have mentioned farmboys, and tornadoes, and manhandlers in one breath, but then there wouldn't have been room left for the tomatoes, mayonnaise, and toasted bread, so we omit them.

Like they call the "Sleepy Room" and lock the key and throw and throw away the door, that poetry is immortal. We plunge and thrash about, about it all. The one whose legs are skin and ones whose bones are black and blue from the shiny white thoughts that cloud on the horizon, like a statue, or a broom pushing a bird. All thought escaped my conscious mind. The bleak bleak cast and there the muscles break, go halfway down the shore and then divide them.

Nothing not the key not the poetry or the sandbags under the eyes of the ivory standing sandman made of ice who hugs the tangerine rainbows never under his arms throws them out over the water of sight into the oblique reflections that the night envisages with its circuitous meanderings of sleet-sheeted eskimo-pies for entering the race of athletes' diamonds' footings In the gazebo of slim grace who drills a hole to the other side and knocks it out with hammers made of legs of chairs with wheels on them that flake to the touch of the slightest wisp of kitchen cleaner bon ami my eyesight is poor as cream is rich in the Hamptons and the oversight of cartwheels in the grave hold tight to woven dreams of seamless bother.

Because of the way they are attached to what they are attached to, the sounds float sideways, not letting up, it moves in loops this way and attracts sympathy where there was only lettuce. The harbor of what I was also thinking of tends to foam at the mouth of men who wet their secret charms of Ocean City. The waves that wash ashore created sand dunes in Ocean City. The saunas that melt manikins into puddles of plexiglass, turn door-knobs to vandals in Ocean City. The tunes of discontent vary little in clambaked Ocean City. There is no comparison between it and Arrow Park except that one eats and sleeps and swims and both exist between the same and vital sun. There is no schav or borsht in Ocean City. The threads that connect have been clipped in Ocean City. Bella Abzug lost the race for mayor here in Ocean City. I love to lick the fingers of all the boys and girls in Ocean City. I am a butch swagger in Ocean City. I am Joe Brainard in Ocean City. I am Edgar Casey In Ocean City. I am Fiorello LaGuardia in Ocean City. I am Ray Johnson in Ocean City. I am a desert of penises in Ocean City. I wait for no one in Ocean City. Be prepared to scream for help in Ocean City. I am a parcel of van strivings tied.

Then. They break out of their molds. They open. They flower into dances. Drawn across in circles. In the motion of destiny that rules the harbored place we call our home. The envelope that surrounds us. We open and lick the pages shut—de-cut the already cut pages back together again. The water that moistens, loosens the bounds of indecisiveness. We are an early look at potatoes in an expressionistic glare that is muted by the frosted finish on the lights that illumine our faces in the dark. We open our minds with a safety pin. I pull on you, you push on me. These other people look at each other's navels. Like olives, they de-pit each other. The night encloses wetness in the rain that dries ill fruit to cactus in rabbits of clay. We wet them till the water comes out the bottom where the hole is. The glory of morning is enhanced by the aroma of French toast that is not there. I think of things and then put them away like soiled laundry. The whiteness of the sun that blends sorrow into syrup for the pancakes which are also not there.

This is as fish that run through the waters—we are exclaimed! We are open to the floodgates of heaven. Tell me again, the thoroughfares that empty every walk of life into another who wakes at the singing of a voice from the street through the window that sits on the wall of the longest sentence in the world which has not yet begun to be written, even.

Well, I walk around what I am going to talk about; why? Because: lights, camera, action—The most beautiful girl in the world isn't Garbo; isn't

Dietrich . . . a balloon that fathoms the inner tubes of prestidigitation—I am no ventriloquist when it comes to acknowledging the falling of the leaves that is "E" as in "Edward."

Don't pull the guilt that sits by a string in the throat of the perceiver who waits to speak about French novels in the grass so green my fine fine peach persimmon pomegranate pear I want to swallow you whole and nibble your cherries I want to milk you lovingly, lasciviously, in the worst and best ways in the worst and best of times I want to pluck your mosquito.

The rain—in the surprise of the absence of rain we ran runningly through the holy lack of emptiness; within parked cars in plastic coats encased—there are no numbering devices for words so short to order, my love—I'll play Cupid to your Guinevere my Lady Godiva let me eat your chocolate melt in my mouth.

My hands are feathers—I move in circularity around your budding eats; forgive what might seem vulgar, it is only suspended enthusiasm over meeting someone I thought I'd never see again, and had no hope, though certainly desire to do so.

You live on a river—a water-way that moves through

flesh. I'll call you, and may the sound of my voice be tenderly received, and the tiny thumping fingers of night that beat upon the drum of dreams, are heard, as through a distance in the jungle, over deserts, mountains, glaciers, impossible seas of distant planets, let me be extravagant!

I am in awe at the stars that I can see through the ceiling of my room in the sky. I am a little snowflake, who grows into a redwood and melts in your hand. I am filled with inflation—with ozone that I must breathe deeply to contain when the thought of you pursues me—I'm a goner.

The "this one" of the poem is you. The poet dreams and pours water over his images like tofu in a bowl in the refrigerator. Ice water. Cubes that melt.

You sit in my lap. That is poetry. Anything else is satire.

The healing voices that descend from the mountain caress us. We sign our name without looking.

The light of light is blinding, and refreshing; like a chocolate chip cookie we have wanted for days—we throw off the sheets in the middle of the might when it gets too hot and extra consonants remind one or Argonauts, or olives that are pitted or not pitted.

We continue, after a fashion, and she wakes up and reminds us that life is still there; we know it is.

We know it so well, we call out in the middle of the night to contain ourselves after a fashion.

Imagining someone is calling our name, we give up—and forget it instead; we make soup and clean up the potatoes and call out the window.

We let down the keys and refrain from speaking. Too often the wind blows away seeds toward the Alps or Adirondacks.

Small insects crawl up our legs in the turmoil we forget ourselves in the light of the full moon.

But death is impressive. It is the lightning flash of the sun-burst in terror that blooms in the face of distortion.

The flowering roses that fall in the springtime catch fire from the tips of their tail-feathers slowly divulging incipient queries to the nature of night-sounds that blow through the shells of the sea that co-mingle rare bread and white water with farthings and welts from the seasons of change that inhabit the growth of apostolic creeds in the city where blooms are discouraged and whitewash excessively governed as lightning disintegrates space at the drop of a pin.

We walk through long hallways to get to the end which we see without seeing, we know what we're in for—look in and look out.

Standing on stone; the water flows between, and someone goes elsewhere. There is a way of proceeding accordingly. According to plan. As though someone were calling your name, unexpectedly, from the street below. But no one does.

You sit. As always. And the night which is life in disguise is punctuated by the sound of the clock that ticks, clockwise, on the shelf. The semicircular canal through which the blood of sound flows.

Asymmetrical as autumn, the real whodunit as the pepper grinds the ground into that voice which exists in our minds alone, as the air is not capable of carrying it.

Where we lived, one crossed the road to get to the other side of it. There was a store there with ice cream and canned goods and cookies and milk and postcards with pictures of the town hall and library taken long ago.

And then you walked back home and sometimes lingered to listen to the sound of the river flowing beneath the bridge, or else detoured down past the feed and building supply store to where the water fell down the waterfall and made great waves and white foam in the night.

You could sit there looking at it forever. And the night would be cold around you but it was nice there. There was where you were then, and that was all there was. You could look around you and hear the sound and see the long-abandoned buildings that had long since gone to ruin, overgrown as they were with weeds and vines.

Like some ancient Greek temple, you could sit there and wonder or close your eyes and imagine you were somewhere else. And you were. Or dream of fixing this place up into a villa by the waterfall. Everyone thought you were crazy. And you were, but you were quite sane, nonetheless.

Walking up the road the sound of the river faded back into the distance and the air was clear again. The streets were so quiet there at night, absent of farmers and workmen coming in for supplies, talking loudly with strong accents and wool clothing worn well from the work that was their livelihood.

No, it was quiet now at night, not like in the city where there was always a sound or someone walking around doing something or other. No, you were the only one out. Your nightly walks you waited for all day. They eventually aroused some suspicion: no one walked around at night, after all, what reason could there possibly be for doing so? You found one, you always found one.

Perhaps it was in place of having someone there to go to or come home to or take home with you. There was no such person. That made things hard sometimes.

The way the other includes this sense of fullness, Yes! This is that other way around where the moon again it is an image a mirage a mirror like self-indulgence which is more particular and allows no faulty grim-faced measures he returns two keys to turn the face away of the article abandoning clock Kathy says that poetry is language and prose includes the rest of the world, I say that prose is long or lengthened, or line-less or continuous unbroken poetry. The time is stopped. Three minute eggs. She observed how I ate boiled eggs in the morning, while not liking them. This is Mary Anne, not Kathy. And then her telling me about telling a mutual friend of ours that I do eat boiled eggs for breakfast without liking them and his wondering whether we just happened to eat breakfast together. The mind functions abstractly, clinging to tangible events instinctively, to hold onto, to wrap itself around. I was industrious. It's seventeen degrees outside. Thank God the heat's on.

I leave a party suddenly without letting anybody know. I hop into a cab and go home to write. I eat dried figs, moist and sweet, almonds and cashews with hot mint tea. If there is one thing that has sustained my life over the past ten years it is mint tea, constant, soothing. When all is said and done, there's nothing like it. Drinking mint tea up in the studio in Vermont while typing up my poems in the loft. Drinking mint tea in Brooklyn, looking out onto the backyard and typing up my poems. Drinking mint tea in Chelsea while looking out onto the backyard and typing up my poems for the first time. Drinking mint tea in Vermont in the kitchen and looking out onto the neighbor's front your and typing up my poems. Drinking mint tea in the attic where I wrote in Vermont and looking out of the door that opened out onto a view of the backyard and the houses on the hill behind it.

The dust and the mint tea. There are memories that never leave, they do not go away. We sit, and write them down. Frogs in the pond. Tadpoles and bullfrogs. Night peepers. Peep. Stars in the sky. Walking down the road. Standing in the night. Looking up. Listening. How the sounds surround you. You move with them. That is, your hearing moves with the sounds it hears. Remembering the smells. The way the air smelled that night. And that night. The color of the sky. The absence of articles in language when we think. The absence of punctuation. The absence of spelling or written culture. Oral transmission. Transmission of mind. Tearing the book. Buddhist sutras. Gleaming lights. In the darkness. Sands awakening. People with the same names. Underdogs of the earth. Standing still. Decyphering. A letter opening the throat. Opening thought. Pulling together. Eating. Love. Toothpaste. Roller coaster. In the wind. On forever. Boots. Rolling away. In the casket. Blind date. Someone is dead.

Propertius. H.D. Chloroform. Chlorophyll. Look at eyes. Girl on the steps. Girl in laundromat. I never said to get me. Together. Always. One word. About fixation. Open again. Loosen.

There it is the bringer of peace and the door that one delicately dared to open, salvaging plants at the last moment possible, creating reality through one's vison of experience, we wind the clock that sits on the mirrored table hoping people got them in the mail the next morning or yesterday, whichever is sooner.

The last vestments of the last eggs we opened and ate (love is a fertilized egg) we sucked through a hole, and which she balanced on the same mirrored table. "One must have a mind of winter/ to regard . . . the pine-trees crusted with snow." The chocolate lilies that grow by day and are eaten by night, that close when they open and reverse the procedure at will; we add an extra "e" as the moment suits us, we cater to our fancy, and chop mushrooms for the omelette.

We put everything into the act, and throw our skeletal system out of wack in doing it, so there are no misunderstandings, we take a bus from Rutland at 6:00 in the morning exiting quietly from Boothbay Harbor which is not far from the interior and Minnie's restaurant in Paris, this is Maine, not France—Those all-night journeys by truck to the coast and the sunrise over the hill—the silent presence of blueberries hitchhiking by the side of the road, or rather, walking along it, eating this breakfast (or another later on in Perkins Cove in Ogunquit), sleeping the night in an abandoned shed on hay or straw I collected outside to make a bedding of, occasional cars going by that sensibly would not stop to pick me up hitching in the middle of the night from Vermont through New Hampshire to Maine, the clock ticks upon the table, a distant dog barks away at the night, sitting up in bed, having overcome the sense of pain in my bones from unnecessary muscular contractions, self-inflicted; I relax somehow, and go to sleep.

He says, "Why doesn't he take his boots off already?" talking to himself. He repeats himself over and over again for his own benefit, and for the benefit of those who might be listening. He itches: it is a sign of life. He is in a bad way. One might not notice it at first, but the signs become apparent rapidly enough. One watches for them. In the darkness of the night one watches for them and types them up as they come along. This is the way the fog breaks. This is the way they break the set. Someone calls out a name: it is not his; he answers anyway, "Anyway!" There is no exclamation point and it is cold. The instinctive difficulty of spelling simple words. Words are knives in the dark. They slice the chain of thought that pursues the thinker in the dark. They haunt the alleyways and moth-eaten places, where no one goes, except by accident.

He puts life on hold: I'll call you later. No one is there later. This is disorienting. This is disconcerting. This gives you heartburn. Take it back. Take it back because the fog broke. Take it back because my arms are hurting. Take it back because it is insufficient. Take it back or I will refuse to recognize you in the future. The future is a bird's nest in my eye. The future is an anticipation of the past. The future is an enclosed rainbow from the start. From start to finish. Here we go. You're kidding me. I fall from the stars. I fall from the stairs. The pleasant click of the keys. And then the noise of the afterward. You said that. You noticed what I meant. You forgot my name. You closed the door. You emptied the garbage. You forgot about it. You left the door open. You shut the window. And then closed it again. You were unconventional. You were magnificent and opulent. You stood in no one's way. You turned the corners of thought down the street until it caved in at the end. No one knows who you are. No one knows who I am talking about. Know one knows knows who you are. No one knows who I am talking about. No one knows the difference between "I before E" and "except after C": or "when sounding like A as in neighbor and weigh." Okay. Forget me not. Petunia.

The insulating angel. The old man with the egg stains on his lapel. Egg yolk on herringbone tweed suit. Semi-tattersall shirt. Maroon tie. Generally disheveled look. Unsteady appearance. Shaky desk. Getting off the subject. Need solidity. Internal and otherwise. Muted from the bottom. Towel-like in appearance. With an A for effort. And E for effort. For effect. The effect of the symphonic repertoire on the twentieth-century consciousness. He doesn't care. It is starting early tonight. They shaky rattle and roll of the legs. We sit on it. We wear it well. It needs this attitude. The attitudes. The attributes. The internal monologues of a first-rate mind. The wanderings of Oedipus. The vast desert of the opera-house. Cymbeline. Watches from the window. Watches from the night. The spaces from the Antipas. Don't don't waste don't waste time on it.

The sounds of spring and the boys in the street. Backspace. They all came to it. They all came to. They all came. Profusely. The windows are made of glass. Maid of glass. How certain of my novels wrote me. Do tell. Margination. The ends of lines. Learning to capitalize letters. Staying home Friday. Larry Richardson. Mentioning names. Finally meeting someone. So easy to know. So and so and so. The dripping water that drips in various places at the same time. The same moment. Saying everything at once, or at least sequentially. Continually beginning. And endless prelude that does not disintegrate into dust. The paraphrasing angel. He always takes a great interest in our young men, our boys who work here. The pink-faced man. He travels extensively and acts as a guide to guided tours to various places around the world. He is always going or coming to or from somewhere or other. He entertains them brilliantly; has them in stitches on the bus. Ought to be a stand-up comedian, instead sits down.

When the one point of life becomes one-pointed
and focused then there is no more room in the room
no more room in the note-book and we are forced to
write it on the machine instead. We click off on the
keys and try to remember the times of December
instead. Help where are it is we going? Because there
is no exclamation point with which to express this
intensity we must that is I alone must work, work to
push it through the words alone. There is no one else
who can do it for me, don't you see; this may see mere
self-indulgence, but it is actually survival, a matter of
nothing less than that. You go I go we go into churches
we happen to pass along our way and light candles
for each other make wishes put in quarters to turn
on the lights and eliminate unnecessary words as
extraneous superfluities. We hear a violent symphony
that threatens to blow the whole thing up off the face
of the earth like mad like wildfire that is one word the
whole world is become one word the music floats away
into the distance into which the music floats away into
which we fall falling like the leaves off trees or snow
that doesn't stop like some voice on the radio you can't
turn off in your sleep it keeps coming and coming on

and on your boots she put quarters in them instead of your pocket already bulging not with quarters you could put it on the other side to even things out but no you suddenly like the way it feels the constant bulge in your pants the permanent erection of being with her she is so good she is so fine she says the same things to you that you say to her she enables you to write at the typewriter everything you do you are doing for her she told you so and you believe her eternally you believe her fully and you believe her completely totally there is no other there never has been nor ever will be any other than her she is there she is everything there is nothing more there is no need for anything more than her in life.

From the top of the World Trade Center you looked out together onto the world onto the city that moves so fast you learn about each other how to live together how anything is possible you learn to speak clearly to write clearly and when she is there there is no need there is no care. She fills you through and through you want to say it all you want to tell the world about it you want to sing in the street to dance at the top of your lungs to slide run swim leap through life together to move slowly learning about the ways of things in this most intimate of examples of existence together this cosmic comic going coming together in-gathering of thoughts and lives and movements smiles songs convergences that become your way of knowing one another the simple words that come to mind express so perfectly the meaning of things in your comprehension which you reach of life together but what is left now she is gone she is going you reach for your tears she is not there the handkerchief is non-existent the window needs washing the floor is there to stand on the feet remember you some distant user and now where are you where your hand your head those thousand things you know about each other life goes on to Washington with brothers ships to build dances and more dances songs romances?

Well where is there to go Pacific Ocean are you blue and green I have never seen you are you water liquid and salty-soft like memories we shared together as ink is black I write and continue writing I can see you there already before you are there I can see you there before you can even see yourself where you are standing water rising up in the ocean there before you please be careful I send you cigarettes of herbs to keep you off tobacco wanting to keep you alive you are so young you make me feel my youth and my maturity together I drink tea alone as the sun goes down around the downtown skyline the inner city puts on its coat and goes on home from work the lights are on the sun a pinkish glow is casting like some fisherman on his way home from a good day's work and I am here breathing bleak connectives to your heart to soothe my imaginary landscape.

I escape into my thoughts of you my treasure-chest of memory of your smells which inhabit this house like incense you said on the phone you could smell my house while we were talking the world can never know it is wrong to think they could no one can understand the world that two inhabit of themselves why try to make them see they have not eyes to see it tangerines and pomegranates Chinese apples and persimmons light the mind and send me away again in pursuit of you cerebrally I have a moment here alone and send away in thought my self to catch the wind through which you fly to touch the hem of your garment passing by I will be healed my faith is such to take us both along with it we fly away I want to go with you with us and church-bells ring across the street as they do every night at 5:15

the haze is blue the lights are gold on the horizon and you are there in Independence City I remember your arrival here you called me amazing as is everything you do from Connecticut you were coming in an hour I would meet you yes I was happy if you could only know how happy I was I was happier than I even knew.

You arrived the sight astounding when I standing there awaiting your appearance in the archway of the entrance from the platform into the lobby of the station looking for your floppy hat I didn't see you not at first you saw me there before I saw you smiling at me seeing me so clearly sleepy clear through waking eyes we met all smiles dancing held each other closely tight we stood together holding on to life that lives inside us now and always we awakened to the dream become reality we left unhinged two months ago up north it was still there the door was open and we entered. And again you were here we were here we were here the wildness on the streets shut out for a while it is just you and me together baby tonight and tonight is all there is and you know this to be true when I look at you when you look at me that is all there is and life is here inside us between us within us surrounding us over under among between in every prepositional configuration.

We exist with it our love that grows and holds us together wherever we are and today a week later Charlie Chaplin is dead on Christmas Day what can be said we went to Catholic mass on Christmas Eve at midnight in Philadelphia with your parents you seated between them protected and safe in their parental discretion our love among the votive candles and angels of the church they watch over us St. Patrick's in New York and we went there eating pretzels buying medals for St. Michael and postcards to send to people elsewhere we climbed the steps and down again you're allowed to make three wishes for free in any church you haven't been to before and light a candle you mother said we thought you only could make one and paid for me you did because I'd been there before New Yorkers buy umbrellas because the snow is wet and dirty and not pleasant in any real or lasting sense like snow in Vermont where the endless whiteness drifts away as endless as the mind that sees it this is where we live although we are not there and technically I am here and

Come out of the outcome already like herring in cream sauce bake like flakey white-out liquid ink-like moleskin unnecessary disease mink-oil saturates the top to the bottom I'm tripping out on words tonight my

dear I'm tight do you hear me calling you I am a parcel
of vain strivings tied I sit at the typewriter and write
like a writer like a thunderstorm retriever in the rain
in Spain I can't resist I'm not sorry stop and unwrap
the words with me tonight like gifts I send them to you
wrapped up in silver linings for the holiday season gifts
are kidnapped like the nape of your neck which I so
love to lick I liken it to a swan's downy softly spinning
like a spider works all night to conceive her vast reward
among the stars and dewy things are laden with our
minds' projections of them they like calculators in the
breeze contrive to call attention to themselves in spite
of inclement weather we thought we might awaken
with a start and bright and early face the morning
with all we've got to offer stay at home and watch the
windows cloud and peel like bells among the sunshine
while tomorrow we among the more awakened things
in nature's valleys romp the grassy meadows green in
search of meaning I'm so glad I'm home I wish that you
were here of course if you lived here you'd be home by
now or I wish I was there wherever you are alas I am
not

Why am I so sad? It is a habit, I suppose, forming

depression as a guise for fear. Life grabs you by the throat and drags you off into the other room. You run, howling off into the hills. Life becomes a melodrama of secrecy. Nobody knows your name, nobody remembers you. Fear sets in. Fear soaks into you like a sponge absorbs water. You want to emerge from it, but you're trapped: trapped in your own snare. You remember what it was like, life among the green things. You recall a distant sense of your name, of that self you once called "you." Long gone. Somewhere there must be some remnant; some scattered scraps of memory to be found. Waylaid bits and pieces long forgotten, somewhere, by the seashore, in the woods. You search, in an attempt to recover those last vestiges of that life, vanished in thin air.

The mind goes back to childhood, instinctively, to seek out the earliest scenes in which the drama was played out. The warmth of mother's presence, calming and encouraging, ever there for you when you needed her. She needed you as much as you needed her. Her life, a shattered dream in which reality played second trombone to imagination. The piercing, pleasant sense of things around her, humorous, cynical, and sharp, penetrated to core of the apple every time. She was there, vibrant and exclusive. Dignified and determined. Unexpurgated and theatrical.

The confrontation of despair in oneself is undoubtedly the business at hand. One meets the moment head-on. It is like charging, full-force, into a mirror. You bang right into the glass. The window is no longer transparent; it is opaque. You rub your nose in it. What is there to do? (The fragments of glass scattered about the floor.) What remains to be done? Get on with the business at hand.

The waking life continues to persist, refusing to let go its grip on you. The words wait, cramped inside to get out; a constipation of the intellect. Loneliness: perhaps this is the fundamental condition of the human beast. Anything else extends from here.

You are somewhere else we are still there maybe somehow we'll get back that place it all began in there among the mountains and the cold the ever-present sense of the oncoming snow the sky blue and icy-still awaiting us as trees await the spring when sap may run and frozen branches thaw just so in the warm manner do you melt my stagnant heart to feelings full and wholesome and I melt into your touch your eyes hair fingers fill me wholly with your warmth and link my days and nights to one and one another ever filling and refilling as the dawn replenishes day with night's fearful tender juices warm and cradled in my arms you rock and dream unearthly things I stroke your hair this lavish silk brown like mink encircling your white shoulders your long neck swan-like which I fill with kisses licks caresses holding you close my window glass like pine tree palms that sit in sun and open cones and whistle sylph rhapsodic.

Through the wood we run gazelle I skip beside you over logs that fell and mushrooms grey and stepped-on we enroll the mosses to cushion our step club-mosses and sphagnum we run cattails rustling marshes' mud-like sticky grabbing feet within it lifting knees up higher we press on to higher altitudes upstream like salmon swimming home to spawn our own young hopes in higher climes we race against time's swift stop-watch ever ticking we race upward to the heights through glaciers melting space resisting higher toward the summit we scale the rocks and crannies the tall unthinkable places where the air is thin we gasp for breath and pause by mountain stream replenishing strength and quenching thirst we wend our way past ferns of bracken there and Tyche helpful by our sides we emerge into the open airy spaces which we sought coniferous rich and barren in its fullness we arrive into the sunshine of that day where we together holding hands become as children again re-enter the Garden of Eden.

"In Advance Of The Broken Arm." Life is an anticipation of disaster. This is the way any intelligent person proceeds. One must live in premonition of what lies around each curve in the road. "Follow your nose." Thus the Sphynx might have addressed Oedipus.

The power of defensive thinking, or how to keep insanity at bay. Thus, the intelligent person is prepared for the worst, at all times. In this manner, one could at best be pleasantly surprised by an unexpectedly advantageous occurrence, or at worst, have one's sensibly pessimistic suspicions fulfilled.

This life is too short for beating-around-the-bush existence. One must "get on with it" continually.

And life is unlocked like a faucet on the sink that leaks water through the stem to stem the tide of thanksgiving where we liquefy our thoughts and leave spaces between spaces to give air our minds to breathe through when they can. Life eliminates the necessity for speech; "You know what this means," means exactly that. The "self" in "self-referential poetry" is the poetry "itself."

You lock up your excesses in the unexplained terrain from which you came, rhythmically, up the stairs one rainy, painful night, desperate and full of excesses. I look at you like an envelope, flowering in your enthusiasm, severe, against the background of the neutral, unnecessary world. The swords break against the water that leaps up, flattened, like a rose tattoo on an arm that is leg-like in its enthusiasm.

You float like an envelope, and antelope in the Bay of Fundy. Unlikely you would be conscious of your existence, which fills a function like milk in the lives of calves, to someone human. The spoon hangs precariously over the edge of the table on this tender night when I eat fire with a fork and knife up my existence with a toothpick like a hawk. I sit, awaiting the moon in my throat, to gag on it. To feed the fire, unquenchable, I bite the dust, like a movie; rip celluloid, sharp beneath my fists, distant, and proverbial. Like sawdust, I am scattered across the floor in handcuffs. I roll down the hill where I lived and the grass was green once. I told you a story. It is painful for me to remember things. I cannot forget them.

You asked me to explain: it is all trying to forget, and remembering instead.

MICHAEL COOPER was born in 1952 and raised in Queens, New York by an artist father and a poet mother. Upon age 17 he ventured forth to the East Village, where he quickly became immersed in the world of the arts. He attended the High School of Music and Art and New York University, from which he received the Thomas Wolfe Memorial Poetry Award. Michael was a frequent reader at the Poetry Project and other venues, as well as being a performance artist associated with the Fluxus group. An early disciple of John Cage from age 16, he served as personal assistant to the publisher, Dick Higgins (Something Else Press), and also to the poet Jackson MacLow. Michael was also Poetry Director of the New York Avant Garde Festival, as well as serving as assistant to the director of that festival, Charlotte Moorman. He was also co-editor of EAR Magazine. He went on to earn degrees from Hunter College (B.A., magna cum laude) and Union Theological Seminary in New York (M. Div.). Michael is a retired Episcopal/Anglican priest, having served parishes with a focus on contemplative spirituality. He also had a career as a professional cellist, performing with local symphonies. He is a committed philosophical Taoist, and is the father of four children. Michael is the author of 17 books of poetry and an experimental novel, *Reap Violet Hiss*. Michael and his son live in Northeast Pennsylvania in a quiet, small town with a cat and two birds and several lovely green plants.